JULY, 1925

PRICE 1/- NET

The Boy's Own Paper

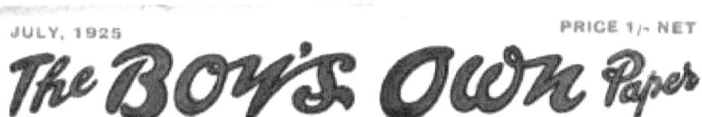

THE WORLD'S BEST MAGAZINE FOR BOYS.

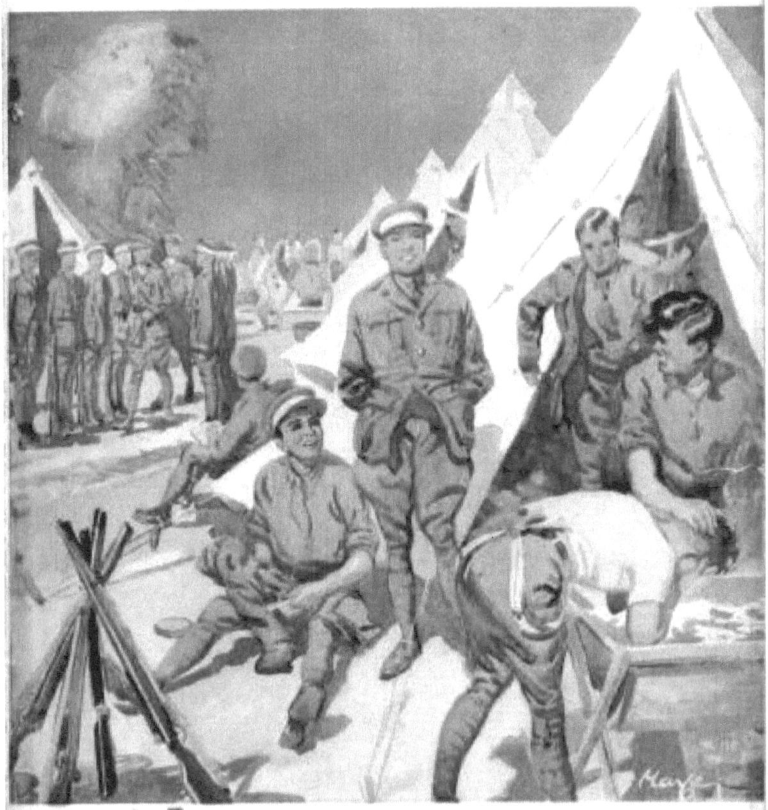

CONTENTS

Copyright

ISBN 9781925281712 (pbk)

ISBN 9781925281729 (ebook)

Boy's Own War is a work of fiction. Any resemblance to real persons, living or dead, is purely coincidental.

Acknowledgements

Jane Sexton for the toughest yet most thorough edit I have experienced.

My wife, Anna Shearer for tolerance.

JUST A BOY

He left home
To fight with men
Just a boy
Won't come home again

In the mud
In Flanders Field
He fell too soon
But did not yield

A boy so proud
To die a man
On foreign soil
Was not the plan

But fight he did
Until his death
The poppy remembers
His last breath !

Carolyn McAllan 21.9.15

Introduction

This book is about war; so how do we define war?

"War is a state of armed conflict between autonomous or coalitions of such organizations. It is generally characterized by extreme collective aggression, destruction, and usually high mortality. The set of techniques used by a group to carry out war is known as warfare. An absence of war is usually called peace.

While some scholars see warfare as a universal and ancestral aspect of human nature, others argue that it is only a result of specific socio-cultural or ecological circumstances.

In 2013 war resulted in 31,000 deaths, down from 72,000 deaths in 1990. The death toll in 2014 would be even greater with the wars in Syria, Iraq and northern Africa raging. The deadliest war in history, in terms of the cumulative number of deaths since its start, is the Second World War, with 60-85 million deaths, followed by the Mongolian Conquests. Proportionally speaking, the most destructive war in modern history is the War of the Triple Alliance, which took the lives of over sixty per cent of Paraguay's population.

In 2003, Richard Smalley identified war as the sixth (of ten) biggest problems facing humanity for the next fifty years. War usually results in significant deterioration of infrastructure and the ecosystem, a decrease in social spending, famine, large-scale emigration from the war zone, and often the mistreatment of civilians.

'Total war is warfare that is not restricted to purely military targets, and can result in massive civilian casualties'

Wikipedia

This definition does not mention children, however, since time immemorial, children have been fighting alongside the grown ups. During the age of chivalry, Pages as young as ten followed their masters into war particularly during the Crusades. Drummer boys marched in front of Napoleon's armies, as they did leading the British into battle. Both the Union and Confederate armies also used them extensively during the American Civil War.

The First World War saw the first wholesale use of children, boys as young as twelve were fighting in the trenches.

It is estimated over 700,000 boys under the age of eighteen fought coming from all sides, with over 100,000 dying in the "War to End all Wars".

Although the same participation rate was not as great in the Second World War, many still fought, particularly from Germany. Hitler used his "Hitler Youth" as cannon fodder when the Russians were invading Germany and ultimately Berlin. It is estimated that close to 30,000 boys and girls lost their lives trying to defend Germany and their Fuhrer.

So now that the world has learned from these ferocious wars and we have become much more sophisticated and knowledgeable does child exploitation in war still go on? Yes, unfortunately more now than ever before.

The use of child soldiers is far more widespread than many can believe; current estimates are that over 300,000 children under the age of eighteen are fighting with machine guns and machetes in war zones around the globe.

It might be argued that eighteen isn't that young, however the average age of these warriors is twelve. So far, the youngest captured fighting in Uganda was five. In Columbia a terrorist bomber was captured, he was seven.

It's not just boys fighting, 30% of the armies employing children also use girls, these girls are being used to fight in approximately fifty-five countries around the world.

A frightening statistic is children currently serve in 40% of the world's armed forces, including rebel groups and terrorist organisations such as Boko Haram and I.S.

It's not just in the war zones where children are exploited, up to half a million children are serving in the armed forces of countries not currently engaged in war.

These kids aren't flocking to recruitment stations, they are being abducted from their villages and forced to engage in unspeakable atrocities to harden their resolve.

They then partake in raids where whole villages are either massacred or kidnapped. The boys are converted into terrorists and the girls into sex slaves.

With an abundance of child recruits, warlords are more prevalent to initiate new conflicts - their supply chain is never-ending.

The legacy they leave behind when these conflicts eventually end are battle-scarred children who require re-education and counselling for many years.

Boy's Own War is a book that will shock you but hopefully also educate you to the horrors of war and the effect it has on our greatest assets... the children.

Explanation of Ranks and Infantry Organisation

Throughout this book terms will be used which may be unfamiliar to the reader.

Infantry Groups

Platoon	24- 48 men comprising 3 to 4 Sections
Company	120 men comprising 3 to 4 Platoons plus HQ support.
Battalion	700-800 men comprising 3 to 4 Companies plus HQ support.
Brigade	3000-4000 men comprising 3 to 4 Battalions plus HQ support.
Division	12000-14000 men comprising 3 to 4 Brigades plus HQ support.
Corps	30,000-40,000 men comprising 3 to 4 Divisions plus HQ support

Infantry Ranks

Private	Basic rank.
Lance Corporal	First possible promotion from Private.
Sergeant	Second in command of a platoon.
Staff Sergeant	Administration
Lieutenant	The most junior commissioned officer, usually commands a platoon.
Captain	Second in command of an infantry Company.
Major	Commands an Infantry Company.
Lieutenant Colonel	Commands an Infantry Regiment.
Colonel	Commanding officer in an Infantry Battalion.
Brigadier	Commands an Infantry Brigade.
Major General	Commands an Infantry Division.
Lieutenant General	Commands an Infantry Corp.
General	Commands an Infantry Army
Field Marshal	Commands many Infantry Armies

School Days

Chapter 1

Melbourne, Australia. 2013

Twenty young boys, all members of the Bentleigh Football Club were standing around in a circle, a huddle formed around their coach Ron Hardeman. They were down the northern end of the Bentleigh Football ground, Ron was giving his final pep talk before the whistle blew and the game began.

> 'OK lads, you know how critical this game is. We win this one and we're into the grand final. It's a must-win game. We have to slaughter them. 'So', he paused. 'What are we going to do?'
>
> 'We're going to kill them,' shouted the team.
>
> 'Are we going to give an inch?'
>
> 'Never. Take no prisoners.'
>
> 'So get out there and show them what you're all made of.'

Joshua Bowes was fifteen, proud that he had made the Bentleigh under-sixteen team playing centre half forward. If it was a good game, he and the other forwards would kick plenty of goals. His best mate from school, Cameron Davey, played for the opposition team, Brighton. It was sometimes a little strange that he and Cameron played together on the firsts team at Haileybury College, the school they both attended, yet here they were sworn enemies, each team fighting for the honour of the grand final.

The umpire's whistle blew signalling the game was underway. The ball was bounced, the ruckman flew, the ball was punched to the Bentleigh centre, Jason Smith, who kicked it to Joshua. He took the mark. Too far out to attempt kicking the goal himself Joshua passed the ball to Tyrone Wright who marked it thirty metres out from goal. Known for his kicking accuracy, Tyrone booted the ball accurately through the posts. Bentleigh had drawn first blood.

The game was fought hard and fast, Bentleigh the victors by twenty points. Celebrations in their change rooms included a somewhat raucous version of the Bentleigh team song.

A markedly different atmosphere in the Brighton room, with heads down, the odd tear and an almost tangible sense of defeat.

Cameron felt miserable. He had so badly wanted to play in the grand final and now had to wait another year without any guarantee Brighton would get through to the top level then. Sounds from the next room became louder as the Bentleigh team ramped up their songs, laughter and celebratory cheers. Cameron's mood sank further. He could only imagine what Joshua would be like when they saw each other at school, full of confidence, boasting to their classmates how Bentleigh had decimated Brighton.

On Monday morning Cameron quietly entered the locker room to collect his books for the day's classes. Unfortunately Joshua had arrived before him, shared the news about his team's big win, blow-by-blow details of the match now being retold for anyone who would listen.

Monday seemed to drag on endlessly as Cameron had to endure the taunting with a brave face, reassuring his classmates that there was always next year. By Wednesday he was his old self again, kicking a football on the school oval with Joshua.

Cameron had decided to attend the final on Saturday, a show of support for his mate and the Bentleigh team.

The big day arrived for this epic contest between the Bentleigh Demons and the McKinnon Lions.

Both coaches urged their respective teams to kill the opposition, wear down the opposition without giving them a chance. The fifteen-year-old boys were instructed to think of the other team as the enemy.

Winner would take all.

The game was fast and furious. Joshua was named 'Best on Ground', an award of little importance as McKinnon triumphed over Bentleigh by one point.

Now the Bentleigh change rooms were silent in defeat, their team's turn to feel completely flat, heads bowed, tears shed as they listened to McKinnon celebrate their narrow win.

Eventually the dejected players left the dressing shed, not really wanting to talk to or see anyone. Cameron waited outside and Joshua finally emerged from the pavilion to see him standing there.

> 'G'day Josh. Well done with 'Best on Ground' mate. Come on, it's not the end of the world. There's always next year.'

> 'I suppose. But right at the moment I feel like shit.'

> 'Well mate, if it's any consolation I know how you feel.'

> 'Yeah, I suppose you do.'

The two friends began their walk home. They didn't talk much but Joshua appreciated the support, sheepishly remembering the way he'd treated Cameron last week.

Final exams were the next important event in their year starting in October. Joshua and Cameron were both sitting for their year eleven certificate, parents and teachers constantly reminding them of the importance of these exams. 'Do well in year eleven and year twelve will be more manageable' or so they hoped.

The two friends studied conscientiously for the exams and passed with flying colours.

'We came off with flying colours.' George Farquar, 'The Beaux's Stratagem (1706). Victorious; extremely successful. The term comes from the practice of a victorious fleet sailing into port with flags flying from all the mastheads. By 1700 or so it was being used figuratively, signifying any kind of triumph

Christmas holidays were the teenagers' favourite time of the year. Cameron's parents owned a holiday house in Torquay, with Joshua's family's summer home at Lorne and a ski lodge in Falls Creek for winter breaks. The two mates wouldn't see each other for four weeks; the absence managed by a love of surfing and meeting girls at local dances in their respective holiday locations.

At the end of January, they returned to school, enthusiastically sharing stories of imagined conquests and the size of waves surfed.

Overall, life was good for these fifteen year olds. No major dramas in their lives and bright futures ahead of them.

The same could not be said about Harry Jordan.

Cricket is War

Chapter 2

Melbourne, 2014

Cricket is a bat-and-ball game played between two teams of 11 players each on a field at the centre of which is a rectangular 22-yard long pitch. Each team takes its turn to bat, attempting to score runs, while the other team fields. Each turn is known as an innings.

The bowler delivers the ball to the batsman who attempts to hit the ball with his bat away from the fielders so he can run to the other end of the pitch and score a run. Each batsman continues batting until he is out. The batting team continues batting until ten batsmen are out, or a specified number of overs of six balls have been bowled, at which point the teams switch roles and the fielding team comes in to bat.

In professional cricket the length of a game ranges from 20 overs per side to Test cricket played over five days. The Laws of Cricket are maintained by the International Cricket Council (ICC) and the Marylebone Cricket Club (MCC) with additional Standard Playing Conditions for Test matches and One Day Internationals.

Cricket was first played in southern England in the 16th century. By the end of the 18th century, it had developed to be the national sport of England. The expansion of the British Empire led to cricket being played overseas and by the mid-19th century the first international match was held. ICC, the game's governing body, has 10 full members The game is most popular in Australia, England, the Indian subcontinent, the West Indies and Southern Africa.

Wikipedia Definition

November 21st 2014

Exams were finished. Joshua and Cameron were waiting for their results with bated breath, grateful cricket season had begun so their minds were occupied with thoughts of fast bowling and playing with a straight bat.

The students had turned sixteen in the off-season with selection for the 'open' team based on ability, irrespective of their age. Unlike football season both boys played cricket for the same team, Moorabbin. With an average age of 20 years among the team, Josh and Cameron knew their work was cut out for them if they were to play with the 'big boys'. Moorabbin was currently the reigning premiers so finding a place in the side would be difficult but not impossible.

Neither boy expected to be chosen now, at the beginning of the season, but serendipity played a hand.

The coach, Phil Montgomery approached while they were practicing in the nets. Joshua was classified as a fast bowler and Cameron a batsman. Despite the pace Joshua was bowling, Cameron was hitting every ball, to both leg and offside.

> 'Boys, could I have a word with the two you please?' said their coach. 'I'm impressed with you both, not only your obvious skills but your work ethic too. I've just heard that Dennis pulled a hamstring earlier, while bowling in the nets. Apparently it looks bad so he's been taken off to hospital to have it assessed. Joshua, how would you feel about stepping in for Dennis when we play St Kilda on Saturday?'

> 'Wow I'd love to Phil. As long as you think I'm up to it.'

> 'Son, I wouldn't have asked you if I didn't think you were ready.'

> 'Well done Josh.' said Cameron, giving a congratulatory pat on his mate's shoulder.

> 'That brings me to you Cam. Ian, our number five batsman, has a nasty flu and had to withdraw. How would you like to replace him in this week's match? And if you prove yourself on Saturday, well you never know.'

The boys grinned at each other as they returned to the nets. An equal mix of excitement and nerves kept them practicing until the coach finally urged them to go home.

October 25 2014

The game was to be played on the St Kilda oval, giving Moorabbin's adversaries a home-ground advantage.

The two captains approached the umpire in the centre of the ground for the coin toss. The St Kilda captain won the toss and elected to bowl. He assessed the pitch as being green, which would aid his spinners and give his fast bowlers some reverse swing.

The weather was unseasonably hot, hovering around thirty degrees; the oval had been watered thoroughly leading up to the game. The outfield would be very fast enabling many boundaries.

The opening batsmen walked to the crease and took their positions. The bowler ran in from the beach end at great speed, delivering a beautiful ball which took the batsman's off stump. The score was one wicket for no score.

The Moorabbin side were four wickets down with only sixty runs scored at tea; not a great start. After tea the batsmen only scored ten more runs when another wicket fell. The game was becoming a farce, Moorabbin were being slaughtered.

It was Cameron's turn to walk to the centre, aware the team's fate was resting squarely on his shoulders.

At the end of the day's play, Moorabbin were 5 wickets for 200 runs.

The following day, Sunday, Moorabbin added another hundred runs before declaring at 8/300, Cameron still at the crease with a score of 175.

St Kilda were 2/180 so Moorabbin needed to do something significant if they were to win this game.

After forty overs had been bowled, the captain called on Joshua. Finally it was his turn to prove himself with the ball.

Josh claimed five wickets for fifty runs. St Kilda were dismissed for 280. Moorabbin had won and now their coach faced some difficult decisions choosing next week's team.

The Spirit of ANZAC

Chapter 3

2014

Joshua and Cameron had previously attended the same primary school, Bentleigh West, before becoming Haileybury College students for the remainder of their school days.

Being an all boys school, great importance was placed on the cadet program at Haileybury, with students in year 11 and 12 all encouraged to enrol. Both boys were enthusiastic cadets; apart from learning etiquette on the parade ground they learnt weaponry, abseiling and many other skills.

Haileybury had a proud tradition for service in the two major wars of the twentieth century. Seventeen former pupils had been awarded the Victoria Cross, three more the George Cross and yet another three the Albert Medal.

740 old boys died in The First World War and another 518 died in The Second World War. The Boer War had killed 55 former students of Haileybury.

As part of the school curriculum all students, not just cadets, must learn about Australia's role in both the First World War and the Second World War. A study of battles the ANZAC soldiers fought, including battlefield tactics, is an integral component of the learning process.

Each year the Victorian Government conducts a 'Spirit of ANZAC' competition, open to all senior schools in the state. Winners, twelve in all, participate in a study tour either to Gallipoli or The Western Front.

Student entries are required to address the following:

The 2015 Anzac Centenary is a time for us to reflect on the Anzac spirit. To what extent do you think it is relevant today? What can it teach us about the Australia we want for the future?

Students are asked to refer to examples of the Anzac spirit from Australia's involvement in wars and conflicts from Gallipoli through to the present day, and relate those experiences to positive values in their community and activities in everyday life.

Entries should be in ONE of the following formats:

- *Essay of up to 1000 words*
- *Poem or short story*
- *Audio presentation (maximum 10 minutes)*
- *Video presentation (maximum 10 minutes)*
- *Digital presentation on CD or DVD*
- *Musical composition – a song or instrumental*
- *Web page or PowerPoint on CD or DVD*
- *Artwork – painting, drawing, photograph or textile*

Non-essay entries require a supporting statement of up to 500 words.

Joshua and Cameron decided to enter the competition as both felt the trip to Europe would be the opportunity of a lifetime.

Creating a sketch of a battlefield scene was Joshua's choice, he decided on The Somme.

The Battle of The Somme by Joshua Bowes

17

Cameron chose the essay option as writing was his forte.

Spirit of ANZAC

By Cameron Davey

I believe that the ANZAC Spirit is still prevalent in our society today, and everyday. Any deed, big or small, can improve a person's life, and everyone has the ability to show the ANZAC Spirit. Whether it's looking after a mate who has it rough, helping others rebuild their lives after disaster, volunteering or even just helping a complete stranger in need.

The media shows many people with the ANZAC Spirit. Yet, I believe the ones who are nameless to the media, are the ones that show the ANZAC Spirit so much more. Large tragedies occur in our world every year, with plenty of media attention.

However we don't see the deeds that go on behind the scenes in local communities, the everyday heroes. For example, Moira Kelly and her acts of humanitarianism. By developing the Children First Foundation, she has changed many lives, and I see this displaying the ANZAC Spirit.

Black Saturday fires and floods in New South Wales and Queensland, are examples of disasters that have left many people to rebuild their lives. The selfless work that went on behind the scenes, to raise money, and to clean up homes was spectacular.

Queensland's Emergency Volunteering initiative is an example of the ANZAC Spirit as any Australian, can help out a fellow mate or stranger, by registering their profession, and if an emergency occurs, you can immediately help.

To me, the ANZAC Spirit has no limits. The way in which Australian and New Zealand battalions risked their lives for our country back in 1915, may never compare with many acts displayed in society today. Yet, we all need to thank these ANZACs from Gallipoli, and the ones still serving today, for making our world a safer place.

Living the ANZAC Spirit can teach young Australians so much about the future that we want. We need a country full of people who care for fellow citizens, who would help a fellow mate or stranger, just out of the goodness of their heart.

It is our responsibility, the future ANZACs to display the ANZAC qualities, to make our country a place where everyone belongs, and where we all feel safe. The ANZAC Spirit will live long in the hearts of Australians, and I hope that it will stay evident in society for the rest of Australian history.

*Essay by Jasmine Davis, College Captain - Sacred Heart College Geelong

Both boys were hopeful but not overly confident. They knew there would be very tough competition not just from within Haileybury but the entire Victorian school system.

Cameron was summoned to the Headmaster's office one Monday morning. He couldn't think of any thing he'd done of late which would necessitate a visit to Mr. Cornish's office.

He was asked by the Headmaster's assistant to take a seat and spent a very nervous twenty minutes in the waiting room before the Headmaster, resplendent is his black robe, beckoned Cameron inside his office.

'So Cameron, you're probably wondering why I summoned you here this morning?'

'Yes sir.'

'Don't look so worried boy. You're not here for punishment but for congratulations.'

'I am sir?'

'You have won the 'Spirit of ANZAC' competition with your excellent essay.'

'Wow, I can't believe it. That's awesome.'

'It certainly is awesome, as you say.'

'Did any other boys from the school win sir?'

'No, I'm afraid not, I would have liked to see more win.'

'Will I get a letter about it all sir?'

'Yes, I expect you will. I'll make the announcement at assembly tomorrow morning.'

Cameron left the Headmaster's office and returned to the classroom. He had difficulty concentrating in English class, his mind was half a world away on The Western Front.

At lunchtime he was approached by Joshua.

'What was that all about? Are you in trouble?'

'Nope.'

Cameron recounted his visit to the Headmaster and the competition news.

'That's fantastic mate, congratulations. I guess that means I missed out. Never mind, I gave it my best shot.'

'You sure did. I thought your sketch was fantastic.'

'Yeah, thanks mate.'

'There's the bell. Suppose we better get to bloody Maths.'

April couldn't come fast enough for Cameron. He was to depart for France on the 11th and start the Western Front battlefield tour on the 15th, the tour concluding on April 26th, the day after the ANZAC Day ceremony.

April 11th 2015

Twelve excited students gathered at Melbourne airport, having met once before when they attended a trip briefing, their chaperones were Ian Jones, Deputy President of the Victorian RSL, and Patricia Jennings, Head Mistress of Brighton High School.

Once on board the plane, everyone settled into their economy class seats eager for the experiences ahead of them.

After what seemed like a lifetime they arrived in Paris via Dubai, where they'd stopped for two hours. The next two days in Paris were for the students to discover the art galleries, museums and of course monuments such as the Eiffel Tower.

The unanimous opinion: Paris was magnificent.

April 16th 2015

The school group caught a Metro train to Gare du Nord where a fast train would take them to Lille and the battlefield tour would begin.

They were accompanied by Gordon Wilson, a senior guide from Boronia Battlefield Tours.

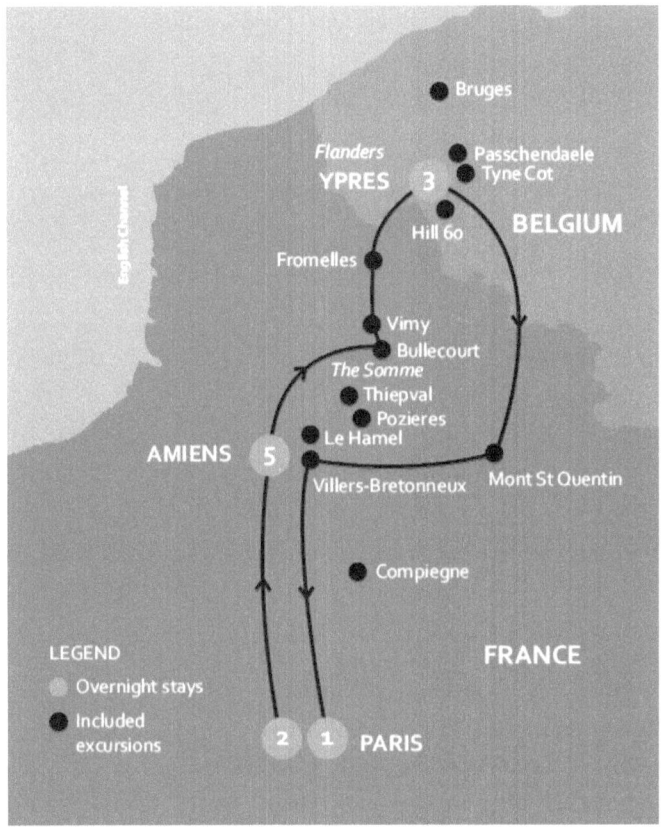

Battlefield Tour Map

Cameron and all the students found the tour both informative and heartbreaking.

Gordon spoke of the thousands of boys, aged fourteen to seventeen years, who had lied about their age and enlisted to fight in World War 1. Many died, including some who were executed by firing squad for desertion and cowardice. This particularly moved the male students of the same age. It could have been them.

Their final stop was Villers-Bretonneux for the ANZAC Dawn Service. The night before the ceremony a copy of the proceedings was distributed among the students.

Official Anzac Day Commemorations 2015

ANZAC Dawn Service

Wednesday, April 25th 2015

Site Opens 3 a.m.

Ceremony Commences 5.30 a.m.

Venue: The Australian National Memorial

Villers-Bretonneux

Villers-Bretonneux Cemetery

Standing in the cold darkness, facing memorial, they contemplated what had taken place a century ago. Not only in Villers-Bretonneux but across the entire Western Front, Gallipoli and the Middle East. Soldiers who had left their homes on their great adventure, only to be confronted with horrible conditions, with far too many lives lost through ill-conceived and badly executed battle plans. Despite the breadth of the First World War, Allied soldiers including the Australian diggers had overcome extraordinary odds and achieved peace.

At dinner, the students and chaperones had discussed how long peace had lasted until another generation was sent away to the Second World War, and then Korea, Malaya, Vietnam, Iraq, and Afghanistan. In total more than 100,000 Australian diggers have died, all in the prime of their lives. In wars occurring since 1860 with the American Civil War, the number of people killed totals more than 175 million, a number increasing all the time.

The sound of drums cut through the darkness and the students' thoughts. The catafalque party slowly approached the cenotaph. The catafalque party consisted of four members of the Australian armed guard who stood, their heads bowed and their weapons reversed, facing outward approximately one metre from the catafalque (cenotaph) as a symbolic form of respect for those who have fallen.

Cameron felt quite special amongst the group, as he was the only one wearing khaki, dressed in his cadet uniform. The ceremony proceeded with the singing of hymns and an address given by the Australian Minister of Veteran Affairs. Wreaths were laid as a lone bugler played the Last Post followed by a minute's silence, later agreed by the students as an incredibly moving part of the service. Reveille was played and the national anthems of Australia, New Zealand, and France. Each student then placed a poppy at the base of the cenotaph.

After the formalities the students and their chaperones made their way to the gunfire breakfast hosted by the people of Villers-Bretonneux. Each year the villagers prepare a traditional ANZAC day breakfast of eggs and bacon with coffee and rum. Mr. Jones and Mrs. Jennings allowed the students a nip of rum in their coffee; after all it was ANZAC Day.

Diggers Gunfire Breakfast

The school group began their return journey with the train to Paris and several hours later boarded the plane to Melbourne.

Opinion was again unanimous; the trip had lived up to all expectations. Their belief in the ANZAC spirit had been strengthened for all time.

Reality soon hit them; ahead was Year 12, their final and most important school year.

Sun Surf & Sex

Chapter 4

November 2015

Joshua and Cameron were seventeen, recently graduated and looking forward to a bright future. They had both scored very well in exams and been accepted into their preferred university courses. Cameron would undertake a Degree in Information Technology while Joshua, joining the School of Engineering, would graduate with a degree in mechanical engineering.

The university term would commence late January and meanwhile the two boys were looking forward to 'schoolies week' in Queensland. Each year, after graduation, thousands of school-leavers from around Australia would descend on the Gold Coast for a week of drinking, drug taking, sex and body surfing. It was renowned as a wild week with police always making many arrests for drunk and disorderly behaviour, not to mention drug possession. In general, most of the kids were well-behaved and just letting off steam after twelve years at school.

Cameron and Joshua, along with four other Haileybury boys, arrived in Surfers Paradise having booked a three-bedroom apartment at the Chevron Apartments.

They threw their bags in the apartment and headed straight for the beach. The weather was magnificent, not a cloud in the sky.

After claiming a spot on the sand they all ran down to the water and dived under the waves, engaging in a bit of bodysurfing. Returning to their towels the Haileybury boys sat and checked out the girls. None of them had seen so many bikini-clad chicks in their lives. Joshua was talking to his good mate Dave about their plans for the night when a stunning girl walked up to him.

'Hey Josh, fancy seeing you here.'

'Oh hi. Sarah. I thought you'd be somewhere on the coast.'

'Of course, I wasn't going to miss out on schoolies.'

'So, where are you staying?'

'At the Chevron Apartments. I'm sharing a place with five school friends.'

You're kidding? That's where we're all staying.'

'No way. What floor?'

'The sixth.'

'That's amazing we're on the seventh. Well, you never know, we might bump into you in the lift sometime.'

'You never know.'

'OK well I better get going. Good to see you Josh.'

'You too Sarah.'

'Jesus mate!' exclaimed Daniel 'Who was that?'

'One of my sister's friends from netball.'

'Well I'd like to bump into her in the lift, or anywhere else for that matter. She's drop-dead gorgeous.'

Two nights later the doorbell rang on the seventh floor. Daniel opened the door. It was Sarah. Daniel was again awestruck. She looked fantastic in a sun frock, just enough cleavage to make him salivate.

'Hi my name's Sarah. I'm a friend of Joshua's. Is he around?'

'Yeah, sure. Oh, JOSHUA. Sarah wants to see you mate.'

Josh was on the balcony sipping a Bundaberg Rum and Coke. He placed the drink on the outside table and came over.

'Hey Sarah, what's up?'

'The girls and I wondered if you boys would like to come over for a drink tonight?'

'Sounds great, what time?'

'In an hour or so, does that suit you?'

'Yeah, sounds fine.'

'Don't you want to check with the other guys first?'

'No need, I speak for all of them.'

'OK, we'll see you a bit later.'

'Done, I'm looking forward to it.'

'Me too, bye.'

The boys were excited. All the girls were stunners, not just Sarah. It became a race for first shower and stealing the best aftershave, which happened to belong to Joshua. By the time Josh came to use the bottle it was half-empty.

Dressed in their best boardshorts and t-shirts, all wearing healthy amounts of Calvin Klein 'Obsession Night', they caught the lift up to the seventh floor and found apartment 72. Joshua rang the bell. Emma, who had been on the beach with Sarah, answered the door. She looked awesome.

'Hi guys come on in.'

Entering the apartment and waving to the other girls preparing drinks and food in the kitchen, the boys all suddenly felt quite shy, not the confident young men of fifteen minutes ago.

Once they all had a drink in their hands their trepidation quickly eased. Conversation flowed and well before midnight everyone seemed to have paired up. Joshua and Sarah were the first to slip away into one of the bedrooms. Other couples took their lead and before long the bedrooms of both apartments were occupied.

The rest of schoolies week was taken up by sun, surf, and sex.

Feeling a Little Piste

Chapter 5

2015 – Winter

Cameron and Joshua had settled into university life; enjoying both their courses and their social life.

The two friends had decided to rent a unit close to Melbourne University; they found suitable digs in the nearby suburb of Flemington. To help pay the rent they both found part time jobs, Joshua in a bottle shop, Cameron in a call centre.

Both students were keen snowboarders, travelling to the snow at every opportunity.

The snow season in Victoria was proving to be one of the best ever. Snow had been falling since the middle of June and by the end of July it was possible to ski in sections not usually available.

The two young men were having a beer on the balcony of their Melbourne unit despite the temperature hovering around freezing.

'Hey Josh, when do you think we can stay in your parent's lodge? I'm hanging out for a bit of snowboarding.'

'Dunno mate, they're up there most weekends. Who can blame them? I'll give Dad a call tonight and check it out.'

Joshua phoned his parents and discovered the lodge was available the following weekend. His folks were more than happy for the two friends to stay. They decided to make it a long weekend away as both students only had one lecture on Friday morning.

On Thursday afternoon they set out on the five-hour drive to Falls Creek, arriving at the lodge by 8.30pm.

The boys didn't unpack, they headed straight for the High Plains Bar to enjoy some schnapps and hopefully meet a few girls.

Although the bar was crowded with young snow-bunnies, alas they both went home alone.

Next morning they woke and peered out of the lodge's full-length windows, it was snowing steadily. They gulped down some breakfast cereal and drank a hot chocolate before setting out on what looked to be an awesome day for snowboarding.

Despite the early hour, the chairlift queue was quite long but fifteen minutes later the boys were making their way to the top of the mountain.

Cameron and Joshua headed off down the run; the snow was good but not powder as there were too many skiers and snowboarders for completely perfect conditions. After their first few runs the slopes were even more crowded.

'Hey Josh what do you think about going off-piste?'

'Yeah I was thinking the same thing.'

'I reckon we do the Maze, it's supposed to be awesome.'

'OK let's do it' said Cameron.

The experienced snowboarders again rode the chairlift up but instead of taking the black run they boarded under the chairlift and over to fresh snow country.

Here the snow was powder. With no beginners to stuff up their runs they had a ball going over small jumps and screaming down the mountain.

Josh was particularly enjoying the thrill of sliding up embankments and jumping natural mounds in the snow. Gum trees were starting to appear above the snowline as they boarded further downhill.

Taking a particularly high jump, Josh lost control landing on the base of a large gum tree. Although wearing a helmet, he hit the side of his neck, hard and lay still in the snow. Cameron was two hundred metres behind and when he came upon his best friend, Josh wasn't breathing. Cameron quickly began CPR and after a few minutes detected a faint heartbeat.

He was in two minds; if he left his mate and sought help would Josh be dead when he arrived back with the medics? But if he stayed with Josh and continued CPR, how would he get them both down the mountain?

Deciding to go for help, it took him twenty minutes to reach the village. Medics raced up the mountain on snowmobiles accompanied by Cameron, their guide to Joshua's location.

Snow had been falling constantly making it difficult for Cameron to find the tree. Finally they reached Joshua, now almost covered in snow. The medics checked his heartbeat and although very faint Joshua was still alive. He was stretchered down the mountain to the medical clinic where they attempted several methods to increase his heartbeat. After sixty minutes of trying the doctor proclaimed Joshua dead.

He was only eighteen.

The Difference Being...

Chapter 6

Joshua died doing something he loved; he wasn't shot by an enemy bullet or ripped apart by shellfire. His generation and the fact he lived in Australia provided every opportunity for Josh to live a full and happy life. It was fate that he died on the slopes of Falls Creek.

This book is about war, yet it's not a novel about enemies fighting to the death or examining the strategies of battles. This book is about young boys, some as young as eight, fighting, killing and being killed.

The first six chapters follow the lives of two normal happy teenagers attending school playing sport and learning about girls.

Joshua dies at the age of sixteen in a snowboarding accident.

The contrast between the experiences of Cameron and Joshua and the other boys in this book is stark. Teenage years are some of the most precious times of our existence, when innocence and bravado are taken away at such a young age it is tragic, like Harry Jordan.

> *"Our youth now love luxury. They have bad manners, contempt for authority; they show disrespect for their elders and love chatter in place of exercise; they no longer rise when elders enter the room; they contradict their parents, chatter before company; gobble up their food and tyrannize their teachers."*

Socrates, 450BC

Teenage years should be spent attending school and learning so that a career can be forged in the later years; a time for playing sport and socialising with the opposite sex. According to UNICEF, 300,000 children are engaged in war today. They are not learning mathematics or science but learning how to be ruthless killing machines. This is a catastrophe that must be addressed by the governments of this world.

Billions of dollars are spent annually on research to alleviate aids, measles, malaria and other diseases that are devastating the earth's children, yet very little is being done to minimise the loss of children's lives in war.

The stories that follow in Boy's Own War will sadden you, shock you and hopefully inspire you.

They're in the Army Now

Chapter 7

London 1914

Harry Jordan was the youngest of eight children raised in a two-story terrace house on London's East Side.

The eldest boy was Henry 19, then came Sam 18, Norman 17, Emily 16, and Joan 15, twins Elizabeth and Margaret 14 and finally Harry 13.

Britain had declared war against the German and Austrian aggressors and everybody in the East End was speculating on what would happen next. Was it going to be a quick and nasty war or would it last until Christmas?

Young Harry worked with his older brothers on the docks, hard physical labour but with little education, it was about the best they could do.

Their father William Jordan was a police officer. He hoped his sons would follow his vocation one day but at the moment there was very little recruitment going on. Victoria, their mother was an intelligent woman who encouraged all her children to read and learn about the world, a firm believer this would improve their lot in life despite any lack of formal education.

Saturday August 15th 1914

The Jordan family were sitting around the dining room table; traditionally the family ate their roast dinner on a Saturday night. After the dishes were cleared, washed, and dried by the children they were free to go off to the local dance or pool hall, depending on their preference.

This particular Saturday night the patriarch of the family made an announcement.

'As you are all aware there's a war going on and the Government has asked all able-bodied men to volunteer. After discussing the situation with your Mother, I have decided that it is my duty to enlist. It is my intention to attend the army recruitment centre on Monday morning.'

'Good on you Father, I think it's very noble of you,' said Emily.

'Thank you Emily.'

'I was thinking seriously of enlisting too, now that you are going I've made my mind up,' said Henry.

'Me too,' said Sam.

'Well Norman and Harry you'll be the men of the household. We expect you to take care of your Mother and sisters while we are away. Mind you, I don't think it will be that long.'

Unbeknownst to his parents Norman had already enlisted, lying about his age. He was due to report to Wellington Barracks on Monday morning.

He decided to keep quiet now and write his parents a letter to be read after he'd left the house.

Victoria was supportive of William going off to war but far less enthusiastic about seeing two of her sons follow him. She resolved herself to the fact and would pray daily they all returned without injury.

Harry went out into the small back yard behind the tool shed and lit up a cigarette he had pinched from his father's pack. It didn't seem fair that his older brothers were heading off to the ultimate adventure while he and Norman stayed at home with the girls.

Monday August 17th 1914

Victoria was in the kitchen making sure all her children were making their breakfast. The girls worked together in the sugar refinery and were due to start at 7.30am. Norm hadn't yet shown his face so Emily was sent to the boy's room to get him moving. Emily returned downstairs clutching Norm's short note that explained he had joined the army and would write soon.

This was too much for Victoria. After the other children set off for work she sat down and sobbed, consumed by fear about her husband and three boys fighting in a horrible war. What if one of them was killed, or God forbid, all of them?

William was angry that Norm hadn't consulted him about enlisting. However he understood Norm's motivation to fight for King and country.

He gathered Henry and Sam and they made their way to the recruitment office. As they approached the building they saw a line of men waiting outside the door.

> 'Looks like we're in for a long wait lads. This war is more popular than I thought'.

After queuing for two hours the Jordan men entered the recruitment office, it was a hive of activity with blokes being examined by doctors and others being measured for uniforms. A tall burly sergeant approached William and asked his age. Without hesitation William lied, saying he was forty-two when actually he was forty-nine.

All three were processed and accepted; delighted they headed to the 'Black Swan' for celebratory ale.

'Well Pa, we're up to our necks now. I hope we made the right decision,' said Henry sipping his pint.

'It's too late to start doubting now son, maybe you should have decided to stay home with your sisters.'

'Don't get me wrong Pa, I thought long and hard before I decided to enlist. It's just a little daunting that's all.'

'I know how Henry feels Pa. It's not that we regret signing up, it's just the thought of killing another human being, Krauts or otherwise.'

'Yeah and trying to avoid German bullets and shells,' said Henry.

'I understand boys, war is no picnic and I'm sure we'll all see and experience terrible things. Now we've enlisted we have to be positive and if you have any misgivings, don't let them be known to anyone, keep them to yourself. Having been a police officer all these years has taught me never to divulge your true feelings to anybody. Others will see this as a weakness.'

The next two weeks were spent getting their affairs in order. As a police sergeant William was released by the force with the assurance he could have his old position back when the war was over.

Although the two boys worked consistently at the docks, they were casual labour so there were no guarantees about future jobs. Henry and Sam weren't too worried as they hoped for better career options when they returned.

August 21st 1914

The Jordan family gathered around the long table for their last meal as a family for some time.

'Well everybody, as you know Henry, Sam and I are leaving tomorrow morning to begin our training. I don't know when we'll all be at the same table again but I'm hopeful of Christmas dinner together. Young Norm has headed off before us. He'll probably greet us when we get to France. Harry, as the man of the house you must look after your sisters and Mother.'

'I think it will more like us looking after Harry and trying to keep him out of mischief,' said Emily.

All the other girls giggled, agreeing with Emily.

'Don't you listen to them Harry I have total faith in you.'

'Thanks Pa.'

'Your Mother has cooked a magnificent bird so let's all enjoy the meal. I've got a strong feeling it will be our last tasty dinner for quite a while, the army isn't known for its food.'

'Don't be getting yourself shot over there Father, we simply couldn't bear it,' said Elizabeth.

'That's right Father keep your head down. We need you back here when this horrid war is over,' agreed Margaret.

'Don't worry girls I've survived as a policeman all these years. A few Germans aren't going to give me any trouble. We'll be fine, won't we lads?'

Henry nodded, 'Of course we will Pa, we know how to take care of ourselves.'

The next day after a tearful farewell, the trio of Jordan men departed for Chelsea Barracks to undergo eight weeks of basic training.

The normal day's regime began with Reveille at 5.30am. This didn't worry William and the boys, they were used to getting up at this hour. The first task of the day was to tidy up and clean the hut, once finished they could enjoy a cup of tea.

Next the focus was improving fitness among the new recruits with marching on the parade ground for an hour and a half. After breakfast the remainder of the morning was spent drilling on the parade ground, learning to march correctly, form fours and about turn. Between 12.15pm and 2pm the men took lunch before returning for more drills until 4.15pm. The unlucky few might be detailed off for fatigues or work parties thereafter but otherwise recruits were off-duty although often required to spend time cleaning kit and shining boots.

'Dad, when do you think we'll be trained on the correct way to fire our rifles and other such things that might keep us alive when we get to the front?'

'Don't worry son, I reckon we've done enough marching. The time for some real training is very near.'

'I bloody hope so, this isn't what I signed up for. And another thing, when do you reckon we'll get our uniforms? I'm sick of wearing the same bloody clothes everyday.'

'You've just got to be a little patient Henry, it will happen.'

Sure enough training soon switched to correct ways to move in the field, including night operations.

Weapon handling skills covered the use of bayonet and hand grenades. Hours were spent practising marksmanship and the correct method to dig a trench; this training would prove very useful when they were at the front.

From 2.30pm on the weekends the recruits played various recreational games including soccer and rugby.

The two Jordan boys were sitting in the mess hut having just finished their dinner.

'So, mate what do you think of army life so far?'

'Well, now that we're shooting rifles and such, not too bad.'

'Do you miss Jane?'

'What a stupid fucking question Sam. Of course I miss her, I love her.'

'Sorry mate, you're right it was a stupid question. Do you reckon you'll marry her when you get back?'

'Yeah, I've got to get back first. Have you read the latest casualty figures? Bloody frightening.'

'What about you? Last I heard you were taking out a beautiful redhead.'

'I don't know, I've got a feeling she won't be around by the time we get back.'

'Why not mate?'

'Her name is Anna. You're right she is beautiful and beautiful girls get taken if you leave them alone. She did say she'd wait for me so, you never know your luck.'

October 16th 1914

At last the day came when William, Henry and Sam Jordan joined the rest of the recruits for the Passing Out Ceremony and graduation from basic training. The Jordan's all became soldiers in the London Regiment 5th London Brigade.

Because William had been a sergeant in the Police Force the Commander of the barracks promoted him to sergeant.

William endeavoured to find out which regiment his son Norm had been posted to but so far his enquiries had been unsuccessful.

Five days leave was granted before they shipped to France. William and his two sons arrived at the family home resplendent in their khaki uniforms.

Their days were spent with family, friends, and sweethearts.

Sam, William, and Henry Jordan

Henry and Sam made the most of their time with their respective girlfriends.

Henry organised a romantic dinner at a little café in East London. They both chose fish and chips with a side salad. Beer was their drink of choice.

> 'Jane, when I return from the war would you consider marrying me?'

> 'Henry, I would be honoured to be your wife.'

> 'Right, wonderful, excellent that's settled then.'

> 'There's only one thing darling.'

> 'Oh, and what's that?'

> 'You've got to come home alive.'

> 'I'll certainly do my best sweetheart.'

Holding hands they left dinner, heads swimming with thoughts of their future lives together.

Sam took Anna to the cinema where the main feature was *The Italian* directed by Reginald Barker.

Anna didn't think much of the film but Sam quite enjoyed it.

They had a coffee on the way home.

> 'Anna do you think we have a future together?'

> 'Well Sam it's hard to say, what with you going off to war and all.'

> 'Assuming I come back in one piece, would you marry me then?'

> 'Sam darling, just come back and then we can talk about it.'

Sam walked her home and kissed her farewell. He was not at all confident that he would ever see her again; Anna could well be married by the time he returned if he ever did return.

William and Victoria lay in bed holding hands both aware they would not make love again for a very long time.

> 'William, promise me you will come home safely. And make sure Henry and Sam are with you.'

'Darling, I will come home unscathed and will take care of our boys. Chances are, by the time we get over there, the war will be over.'

'I certainly hope so. Should I make you wait until your return to make love again?'

'I have no control over how long this war will go on for my darling.'

'That's true, come here.'

The next morning the two brothers said goodbye to their mother, sisters and little brother. William hugged his wife reiterating his promise to return as they departed to join their Battalion at barracks.

October 18th 1914

The 5th London Regiment marched to the dock at Southampton and boarded several troop ships bound for Marseilles.

Conditions were hot and cramped and with many of the men suffering from seasickness it was often a fight to reach the hand railing.

After what seemed an eternity the ships pulled into Marseilles, the majority of the soldiers could not wait to feel the earth under their feet.

Their journey continued by train up to Belgium and a city called Ypres. Most of the troops had never heard of Ypres, let alone pronounce it correctly.

Again conditions were cramped on the train but at least they didn't have rough seas to contend with.

So far the Jordan men had been able to stick together and it was reassuring for Henry and Sam to have their father by their side.

Two days before the 5th London Regiment arrived fighting began. This became known as the First Battle of Ypres.

Ypres October 29th 1914
The Cloth Hall and Cathedral

Troops were assembled at the railway siding ready to march into Ypres. There seemed no visible fighting although they could hear artillery in the distance.

1st London Brigade Marching into Ypres

The Prodigal Son Never Returns

Chapter 8

Norm Jordan arrived in Marseilles on October 2nd 1914, two weeks before his father and brothers. He hadn't enjoyed the short sea journey at all, the ship was cramped and he became seasick immediately the swells began.

He, along with his battalion, The Royal Fusiliers, were then loaded on trains to join their countrymen at Ypres in the Flanders region of Belgium.

Norm, a shy boy who typically found it difficult to make friends, had met and befriended a fellow called James Hargreaves. Despite completely different backgrounds they got on extremely well. James' middle-class family included a father who was a doctor with his mother a nurse. James had also lied about his age to enlist, sharing the same birthday as Norm.

They arrived at Ypres on October 14 at last able to stretch their legs and walk around the pretty town dominated by the Cloth House and the Cathedral beside it.

Sightseeing was soon replaced by the horror of combat - the two boys were about to partake in the 1st Battle of Ypres.

1st Battle of Ypres

On October 19th near the north Belgian city of Ypres, Allied and German forces began the first of three battles to control the city and its advantageous coastal position during this First World War.

After the Germans advanced through Belgium and eastern France with minimal resistance, their great push was curtailed in late September 1914 by a decisive Allied victory in the Battle of Marne. The 'Race to the Sea' began as each army attempted to outflank the other on their way northwards, hastily constructing trench fortifications as they went. The race ended in mid-October at Ypres, the ancient Flemish city with its fortifications guarding the ports of the English Channel and beyond, the North Sea.

Following the Germans capture of Antwerp in early October, Belgian forces and troops of the British Expeditionary Force commanded by Sir John French withdrew to Ypres, arriving at the city between October 8th and 19th to reinforce the Belgian and French defences. Meanwhile the Germans prepared to launch the first phase of an offensive aimed at breaking the Allied lines and capturing Ypres and other channel ports, thus controlling access to the North Sea.

On October 19th a protracted period of fierce combat began as the Germans opened their Flanders offensive. The Allies steadfastly resisted while seeking their own chances to go on the attack wherever possible. Fighting continued with heavy losses on both sides.

The Allied forces suffered 7,960 deaths, 29,563 wounded and 17,875 missing presumed dead. Winter weather forced the battle and killing to a halt. The area on the British side to Menin and Roulers on the German side became known as the Ypres Salient, a region that would see some of the war's bitterest and most brutal struggles over the next few years.

Norm and his mate James were billeted out in a farmhouse on the outskirts of Ypres. The Belgium family who cared for them were very nice although neither boy could speak Flemish or French, the two languages spoken in the house.

On the morning of October 19th they woke to the sounds of loud banging on the front door. Mrs Joossens came quickly down the stairs and opened the door standing in front of her was a sergeant from the British army.

> 'Sorry if I woke you Ma'am but I need to collect the two soldiers you have been billeting. Immediately.'

The two boys heard the conversation and came to the door.

> 'OK lads, time to go. We've got a war to fight and by all accounts your war starts today.'

Acknowledging the sergeant they gathered their packs and said farewell to Mrs Joossens. The two young soldiers followed their sergeant as he rounded up another twenty or so Royal Fusiliers. It seemed they were all about the same age as Norm and James. They marched through Ypres and headed for the line at Langemarck a town north of Ypres and neighbouring Passchendaele.

October 21st 1914

At five in the afternoon the Fusiliers arrived at the front line facing the German army. The British Commanders were expecting a push from the German 4th Army, their task was to stop it.

Norm and James sat waiting in the trench, smoking. They'd both recently started, as every other soldier seemed to do so. Whether it alleviated boredom or calmed their nerves, cigarettes were given to them as part of their rations. They were smoking and silent, both very nervous if not terrified.

Unbeknownst to them, in the opposite German trenches were young soldiers not much older than they were. Nicknamed the 'Kinder Korps', these German university students had been willingly seconded into the army to boost the strength of their country's battalions. The German commanders didn't intersperse these young men among older, more experienced soldiers; they banded them together in the one battalion.

Enemy artillery began to rain down on the British positions. At first their range was inaccurate so they didn't cause too much havoc. However it didn't take long before the Germans worked out the coordinates and shells were dropping in or close to the Allied trenches. Norm and James witnessed their first casualty – a soldier, only ten yards away, received shrapnel to his neck almost severing his head. Both boys were in shock but knew they had to pull themselves together.

Captain McDonald their Commander moved down the trenches alerting troops to the fact that when the barrage ended a charging German army would confront them.

As expected, the barrage ceased. They waited in silence, an acrid smell from shells permeating throughout the trenches. Looking out with a periscope Captain McDonald saw a mist drifting over no man's land. Not a mist as he had experienced in his home country of Scotland, but nevertheless a mist. Smoke from the barrage was making it problematic to see more than fifty yards ahead. He saw movement and faintly made out a row of enemy troops making their way to attack the British line. He quickly blew the whistle to alert his troops of the impending attack.

Norm and James looked at each other and nodded as if to say, we'll be all right, we know how to fight. This composed approach did nothing to calm the butterflies in their stomachs.

The Krauts started to fire their rifles and machine guns were attacking the trenches. In return the Allies began to fire back with rifle, machine gun and mortar. The Germans were dropping like flies but more and more kept coming; it was a bloodbath.

A German soldier managed to reach James and Norm's section of the trench and leapt forward to jump in. Norm held up his bayonet and impaled the eighteen-year-old student soldier from Heidelberg. Withdrawing the blade, Norm then shot the wounded soldier to eliminate the obvious pain he was suffering.

Turning to face the onslaught again, Norm glanced toward James only to find his mate slumped over the wall of the trench. He had been hit in the forehead and would've died instantly. This sight made Norm even more determined. The Germans were beginning to retreat and orders were to go after the bastards. Norm climbed the ladder and began to run, firing his 303 at the retreating enemy. He was confident he had killed a few when a German machine gun ripped him apart.

The first casualty in the Jordan family, his mother received a telegram two weeks later. Norm was just seventeen. His father William was not notified for several more weeks.

Norm Jordan

Private Investigations

Chapter 9

Sergeant William Jordan was sitting in a dugout alone. He had a piece of paper in his hand and kept reading the words over and over but couldn't bring himself to believe them.

It is with great regret to inform you, your son private Norman Jordan was killed in action near Ypres on 21 October 1914.

What sort of world was it that a son dies before his father? The lad was only seventeen for God sakes.'

He would have to try and track down Henry and Sam who had been transferred to the 8th division. He had no idea where they were now located but, was sure he would find them eventually.

A messenger entered the dugout, interrupting William's sorrowful contemplation. The young soldier handed him an envelope. The note ordered William to report to divisional headquarters in a chateau thirty miles behind the lines in Boulogne, where General John French was based.

Instructed to leave for Boulogne immediately, there would be little time for mourning. A vehicle already waiting to take him, William grabbed his pack and left. He arrived at the port city in the afternoon and was shown his quarters, an army tent large enough to accommodate four officers, but in this instance, for him alone.

He ate his evening meal in the mess tent and retired at 9pm.

Reveille was at five thirty, breakfast at eight. William waited around for someone to inform him why he had been summoned, finally at 10am a captain introduced himself and asked William to accompany him to the quarters of Lieutenant Colonel Francis Oats.

'Sergeant William Jordan, Sir,' Captain Harris said.

'Oh good, come on in sergeant, would you care for a cup of tea?'

'Yes Sir, that would be very nice.'

'While my orderly organises things let me pass on my sympathy for the loss of your young son. Terrible thing.'

'Thank you Sir. Yes it is very difficult to accept losing a son so young.'

'Yes, no doubt it is. Now Jordan, I believe you were a sergeant in the London Police, homicide squad I believe.'

'Yes Sir, I had twenty years with the force and God willing I'll return to policing when the war is over.'

'Sterling. I am sure they will be happy to have you back. Sergeant the reason I'm interested in your police background is we've had a terrible murder in Poperinge, a Captain Pittard. He was responsible for the logistics of all goods coming and going at the warehouses. You can appreciate this is a critical role.'

'Are you asking me for some advice on how to go about capturing the perpetrators Sir?'

'Well, I'm asking for a little more than that. I want you to be Captain Pittard's replacement, getting you inside to find the information we need to bring these murderous bastards to justice.'

'You say these, as if there is more than one of them. May I ask what brings you to that conclusion?'

'My suspicion is that a major smuggling ring is involved. Captain Pittard may well have discovered details but before he could report them he was murdered.

Your orders are to report to the Poperinge warehouse as the new officer in charge. I will promote you to Captain, a rank you will retain for the war's duration. There is one catch. We need to make sure nobody knows your background so you will be deleted from all war records and army records. From now on you are Captain Sykes of the 60th London Division. This of course means you will be listed as "missing". Your wife will be informed as such, as will your two sons fighting over here.'

'Is that absolutely necessary sir? My wife and family will be devastated.'

'I'm afraid it is Captain; there can be no argument. The success of the mission depends on it.'

'Yes Sir, when should I leave for Poperinge Sir?

'Tomorrow, you need to be fitted out with a new uniform and such.'

'I take it I report directly to you Sir?'

'That's correct Captain, I expect weekly reports.'

'Thank you Sir.'

'Go and find these bastards Captain, we're all relying on you.'

William saluted and departed for his tent, he had a lot to think about.

Next morning his new uniform was delivered, he had to admit to himself he looked rather smart in a Captains uniform with the three stars on his epaulets.

A staff car collected him for the long journey to Poperinge, a place he had only visited once before. He wasn't very impressed with the troops' drunken behaviour or their propensity to visit the town's famous brothels. However William did enjoy visiting Talbot House, a place where he could relax and chat with other soldiers about their experiences thus far.

Located in the West Flanders region of Belgium, near to the border with France, Poperinge was just behind Allied lines and served as an R&R spot for Allied troops. Allied soldiers knew the town as "Pops". Most of the British soldiers who fought on the Western Front passed through Poperinge. The town served as a major British supply base and garrison for the front.

Poperinge also became the hub for informal social life for Allied soldiers, particularly British troops, during the war. "Pops" provided soldiers with a brief reprieve from the harsh life of the trenches and the front. A thriving black market trade developed, with British military supplies being sold at inflated prices. The town also had numerous cafés, estaminets (bars or pubs) and brothels, which were frequented by the troops. Poperinge was a safe place for British troops and supply depots because it lay just beyond the range of German artillery.

Talbot House

One of the centres of social life for soldiers in Poperinge during the First World War was Talbot House. Talbot House was established in 1915 as a club for British soldiers by Reverend Philip 'Tubby' Clayton and Chaplain Neville Talbot. Talbot House was named for Chaplain Talbot's younger brother, Lieutenant Gilbert Talbot, who had recently been killed in the vicinity of the nearby villages of Hooge and Zillebeke.

Reverend 'Tubby' Clayton was a short thirty-year old vicar in the Anglican Church. He had arrived in Belgium in November 1915 and was assigned to serve as the military chaplain to the British 16th Infantry Brigade. The previous chaplain for the 16th Brigade had been killed the month before.

When Reverend Clayton visited Poperinge he observed that aside from cafés, drinking spots, and houses of prostitution, soldiers had no places to go in the town. Clayton wanted to establish a place for soldiers to gather that was removed from the 'debauchery' that characterized many of the other places that British soldiers frequented.

Arriving at Pops he was driven to a quaint cottage. This was to be his home for the duration of the investigation.

He entered and found a very nice sitting room with a wood-fired slow combustion fire. There was a chesterfield lounge suite in a rich burgundy colour and a gramophone together with a sizable record collection.

This certainly beats the heck out of the dugout I once called home.

Upstairs were two bedrooms tastefully decorated and a bathroom. He looked out the bedroom window and could see a very well maintained garden with a lawn that had obviously just been mown.

This may well be a very long investigation, he thought.

Poperinge Cottage

After the best night's sleep he had enjoyed since joining up, he sat down to a breakfast of fresh fruit and bread spread with lashings of honey.

'Things could only get worse,' he thought. 'I'm sure I will solve this case soon and then I'll be back in the mud. Although I will be a Captain so I will get a few more privileges.'

A knock on the door brought him out of his daydreaming.

'Enter.'

'Sir, I am Sergeant Abbott. I've been instructed to take you to the warehouse complex where your office is located. I am also to show you around the facility and answer any questions you may have Sir.'

'At ease Sergeant. Have you been in this role for long?'

'Since our boys arrived here Sir, that would be September 1914.'

'You reported to Captain Pittard?'

'I did Sir, we arrived here on the same day.'

'What was he like, Sergeant?'

'He was a wonderful man Sir, you couldn't find a finer gentleman.'

'Did he have any enemies that you knew of?'

'No Sir, he was very popular with all the men. Mind you, if you stepped out of line he'd soon bring you back.'

'So, why on earth would someone want him dead?'

'It's a complete mystery Sir, I really don't know.'

'All right Sergeant, show me where I'll be stationed.'

'Yes Sir, follow me Sir.'

The two men left the cottage and stepped into a staff car. The driver was a young private, he didn't look much older than Norm.

They arrived at the warehouse ten minutes later, Sergeant Abbott opened the door for his superior and they entered what would be William's office.

'This looks perfectly adequate. Have you left Captain Pittard's things untouched?'

'Yes Sir, I can arrange for them to be taken out if you wish.'

'No, don't bother. I may find some things that will help me get started more quickly. You know, procedures he used and so forth.'

'Yes Sir, whatever you think is best. Would you care to inspect the warehouses and the below ground munitions store?'

'Yes I would, thank you Sergeant. Lead the way.'

The two men walked into the first storehouse. It was a hive of activity, medical supplies were being packed into wooden boxes ready to be transported to the front. Other supplies such as tinned food and biscuits, tea and coffee were also packed into the boxes for shipment.

They walked into the second storehouse and it was a similar scene, with people everywhere packing rifles and uniforms as well as many other sundry items.

Number One Store House

Captain Sykes asked if he could inspect the rail platform where most of the goods arrived for storage and distribution.

Two trains a day arrived at the landing making the station an assiduous depot.

Not only were the trains hauling cargo they were also used to transport troops.

Unloading Rail Cars

Finally Captain Sykes inspected the underground weapon storage, the most important facility to support the war effort.

'Have there been any accidents while handling the shells etc. Sergeant?

'I'm afraid so Sir, we lose about one or two of our finest every month.'

'Surely we can improve procedures to minimise accidents happening.'

'Captain Pittard tried implementing all sorts of safety measures but to no avail.'

'Well I'm certainly going to try my hardest to reduce these accidents'

'Yes Sir.'

When you think of the numbers we're losing each day on the front, a couple each month pales into insignificance, thought Sergeant Abbott to himself.

'Right then. I think I'll walk back to my office and try and get my head around the operation. I won't need you for the remainder of the day Sergeant. By the way, what do you actually do?'

'I check the manifests against the goods received in store one sir.'

'Are there ever any anomalies? You know, goods listed but not supplied?'

'Not generally Sir, there is a very small amount of pilfering but generally all the goods are present and accounted for.'

William entered his office and sat down at the oak desk; the chair was one that swivelled, he'd never sat in a chair quite like it. On the desk was a silver frame with a photo of a very attractive woman, Captain Pittard's wife or sweetheart he thought. He placed it carefully in the desk's bottom drawer. He looked around the office, everything had its place and was very neat. He was obviously a very fastidious man, he thought.

He got up and opened the top drawer of the filing cabinet; files were in alphabetical order making it easier to find a particular file. William decided that he needed to go through each file carefully to determine if they contained any clues to Pittard's demise.

He grabbed a bunch, A to G, and sat back down at his desk. Most of them were routine manifests for shipments personnel records and various other sundry matters. By the end of the day he had read every file up to T. His eyes were watering and he found it difficult to focus. Time to call it a day, he thought. He rang the driver who came immediately and drove him home to the cottage.

When he entered the sitting room he noticed a decanter, he sniffed its contents, sure enough it was scotch. Bloody hell, the life of a Captain is a charmed one, he thought.

Pouring himself a glass, he sat in the leather wingback and contemplated the day.

Nothing seemed suspicious, nor did any particular person stand out. His thoughts of a long investigation may well prove to be true.

There had to be a reason why one or more parties decided they had to murder Pittard. He had probably discovered a racket or something. Time would tell, he was determined to solve this murder. His nickname in the force was Bulldog.

Bulldog

Chapter 10

Weeks passed with William sending regular reports to Lieutenant Colonel Oats as required but little to really tell. He reported that Captain Pittard was a well respected officer who appeared to have no enemies. Spot-checking the manifests against the cargo hadn't exposed any pilfering. He also investigated whether Captain Pittard had a mistress but by all accounts he remained faithful to his wife back home. Despite the hunch Pittard had uncovered a racket, to date no such racket had been uncovered.

May 1915

Henry and Sam had survived their first combat, The Second Battle of Ypres.

The battle began in April 1915, a German plan developed to divert Allied attention away from the Eastern Front. It was also the first battle where the Germans used chlorine gas. The Allies drove the Germans back to their lines, a failure for the Germans and victory for the Allies. As a result of this unsuccessful attack the German army gave up its attempts to take the town, choosing instead to demolish it by means of constant bombardment. By the end of the war Ypres had been largely destroyed.

Ypres 1917

The two Jordan boys were given leave and chose to spend it in Poperinge. They had witnessed horrible carnage and injury including the effects of the German gas. Both felt fortunate to have survived and were now intent on enjoying themselves for a while.

Henry and Sam were walking through the busy town centre when they noticed an officer's limousine. To their amazement their father William was riding in the back. Yet the boys were still coming to grips with the fact their father was listed as missing, presumed dead.

Sam jumped up and down and waved to his father, as did Henry. The officer glanced in their direction then continued to read the document he was holding.

> 'What the fuck! That was Pa, I'm sure of it,' yelled Sam.
>
> 'I know mate, that was him, for fuck's sake I know my own father. What in God's name is going on?'
>
> 'Let's go to headquarters and see if we can get to the bottom of this' said Henry.

The bewildered young soldiers visited HQ and explained their experience to the officer on duty. Obligingly he checked the records but couldn't even find Sergeant Jordan listed as missing. As far as he could tell there had never been such a person registered in the British Army.

The Jordan boys left the offices dejected and confused. Rather than visit a brothel they decided to get some advice from Tubby over at Talbot House.

Meanwhile William was sitting in his office trying not to weep, the sight of his two sons waving excitably had a devastating effect on him. He was seriously considering calling Lieutenant Colonel Oats and pleading to be taken off the case. He looked down at his desk noticing a handwritten note folded over twice. All his mail arrived in envelopes so this was highly unusual.

He opened it up and began to read.

Dear Captain Sykes,

I can't divulge my identity for fear of retribution, I know what happened to Captain Pittard or I should say I know why they killed him.

Captain Pittard uncovered a crime ring operating in the Poperinge storehouses.

I know you have been monitoring the manifests and checking that all goods listed are accounted for. This has given you a false interpretation.

What has actually been happening is that the manifests are altered en route. Sailors in the merchant fleet are paid significant amounts to forge manifests.

The goods I specifically refer to are medical supplies, mainly morphine. Once the ships are unloaded the 'extra' morphine is stolen leaving only the amount listed on the falsified manifest.

The morphine is then loaded into ballast crates and shipped back to where it came from originally; America. Gangs from New York then sell it either as morphine or heroin a more refined form of the drug. Apparently there are huge sums of money to be made on the black market.

Captain Pittard became suspicious and organised for a military policeman to go undercover as a merchant seaman. It was while this policeman was on board that he discovered the scam.

The gang in Poperinge involves all levels. A fellow officer, one of the gang, informed the leaders that Captain Pittard was about to arrest the gang leaders. They got in first and eliminated him.

I am putting my own life in danger by divulging the gang leaders but I owe it to Captain Pittard and the boys at the front that aren't getting the morphine they need.

The three major leaders are:

Sergeant Abbott

Major Thomas Albright

Corporal Bernard Bennett

Sir I wish you every success in your endeavours.

Anonymous

William reread the letter; astonished that Sergeant Abbott his right-hand man was one of the gang leaders. He had to be very careful how the situation was handled. Abbott had been privy to information and could prove to be dangerous. Although William had not divulged the true reason for replacing Pittard nevertheless…

This letter changed his mind about requesting to be excused from the case. If in fact the accusations were correct, the case would soon be solved and William could return to his family and divulge the truth about his recent role.

He had to decide whether this week's report to Oats mentioned what he had just learnt before actually verifying it as truth. No, it was better not to, as a proven case was far preferable to speculation based on an anonymous letter.

Where's My Dad?

Chapter 11

April 1916 - London

Harry Jordan continued working on the docks while the war raged on and everyone else seemed to be fighting for King and country. When he learned his brother Norm had been killed, he and the rest of the family were devastated.

Two long years had passed since Harry had seen his father and brothers. What if he never saw them again? He loved his mother and sisters but being the only male in the household was difficult at times.

Harry had been contemplating sneaking away to enlist in the army, surely a better chance of catching up everyone if he was over there too.

A final decision was made one Monday morning in April. Before the others woke, Harry slipped out the front door and headed for the army recruitment office. He had a little time to kill before the doors opened so walked down to the Thames and along the bank, taking a seat on a bench overlooking the river, the city of London on the other side. Harry asked himself some appropriate questions such as 'Do you really want to do this?' The answers were all affirmative. Looking at his watch he realised it was time to return to the recruitment centre.

There were only a few other men waiting, a sharp contrast to 1914 and the two-hour queues for enlisting.

The doors opened punctually, a tall skinny sergeant greeted the potential recruits.

> 'Good morning gentlemen. Make your way inside and we'll get you all processed.'

When it was time for Harry to declare his age he responded confidently.

> 'Eighteen Sir.'

The recruitment officer looked Harry up and down.

'Right, well you'll do. Sign these documents and go into the next room to be sized up for your uniform.'

Harry did as he was instructed, the first of many orders he would have to obey throughout his army career.

He felt a pang of guilt about not leaving a letter for his mother, worried she would contact the authorities and reveal his true age. Even with the catastrophic casualties the Allies were enduring in France and Belgium, they wouldn't take a fifteen-year-old boy.

It would be easier to write from the front once he had settled in.

The next stage in Harry's military career was training camp at Chelsea Barracks, the same place his Dad and brothers had attended.

Normally new recruits trained for eight weeks but with the need for reinforcements this was reduced to six weeks. Barely enough time to learn correct marching let alone how to fire a rifle accurately.

June 1st 1916

Harry boarded the troop ship *Esperance* that would take him and his pals to war. They berthed at Marseilles and were immediately taken to the railway platform for the train journey to Poperinge.

The town was abuzz with soldiers; trucks and horses coming and going through the cobblestone streets.

His battalion, the 19th of the London Brigade, were accommodated in a tent city behind the village itself. During their two days in Pops some of the older soldiers frequented the famous brothels but Harry found Talbot House more to his liking. There was a visitor's book, which he meticulously scanned to see if his father and brothers had been there. Sure enough he found entries by all three and reading their entries really lifted his spirits.

December 1914

What a wonderful haven to get away from the war and just relax and contemplate. Thank you Tubby.

Sergeant William Jordan

December 1914

Thank you Tubby, enjoyed the tea and the long chat we had.

Private Henry Jordan

December 1914

I really enjoyed this place Tubby. Thank you.

Private Sam Jordan

Harry was delighted the three other Jordans were still together. They really had been able to look out for each other.

The brigade assembled in the main square of Poperinge to be loaded on London buses and taken to the Somme valley in preparation for a major push against the Bosch.

Leaving For the Front

Everybody felt a real sense of excitement. At last they would have the opportunity to blast the hell out of the Germans.

The trip to the Somme took four days through mud, ice, and snow. It wasn't particularly comfortable but beat the heck out of marching with a sixty-pound pack on your back.

Off to War We Go

Harry wondered whether his father and brothers would be taking part in this same battle. Awestruck by everything around him, huge guns lined the entire front facing the German lines, men were carrying ammunition boxes into the support trenches, horses were hauling Howitzers into position. Soldiers were everywhere he looked, Harry had no idea how many. In actual fact thirteen divisions, around 150,000 men, took part in the first day of the Battle of the Somme.

Front Line Artillery at the Somme

Harry's battalion were ordered to report to Major Thomas at operational headquarters. Major Thomas addressed them, emphasising that the German army would be close to annihilation after the Allied barrage that had taken place for several days now.

> 'Men when you go over the top tomorrow morning, our orders from General Haig are to walk purposefully. We do not run. The likelihood of encountering strong defence is minimal. You may encounter sporadic fire but it's likely to be minimal. Your commanders will lead you to your positions in the trench. I wish you God's speed and may you live to fight another day.'

Moving in formation the men from the London area marched about a mile to their section of the trench opposite the objective, Gommecourt.

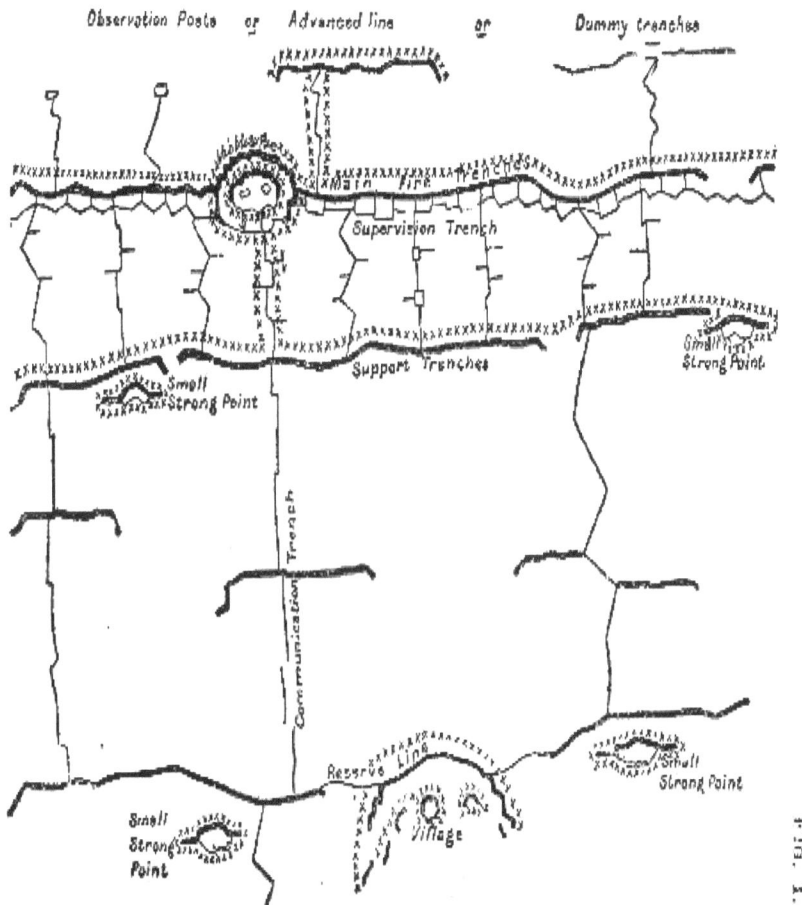

ARRANGEMENT OF DEFENSIVE LINE

German Defence Line: The Somme

Typically trench systems consisted of three main fire or support trenches, connected by communication trenches, various posts, strong points, and saps used to tunnel underneath the enemy lines and detonate explosives.

By 1916, the German system of defence had three or four such trench systems layered back over a distance of a couple of miles.

By 1917, the system had deepened even further.

The assaults of 1918 faced defensive systems several miles deep.

June 30th 1916

Noise from the big guns made sleep virtually impossible. Everyone tried to be indifferent to what was going on around them but actually they were all petrified.

'Hey Harry, we're about to put our lives on the line for King and country. Isn't it time you told us just how fucking old you really are?'

'What do you mean? I'm eighteen just like you Frank.'

'Bullshit Harry, fifteen if you're lucky.'

'I've always looked young for my age mate.'

'Yeah right.'

'Anyway it doesn't matter anymore. I'm here and that's that.'

'Fair enough mate.'

'So Frank what do you think about tomorrow? I mean our leisurely stroll across no man's land?'

'Mate if I've got Gerry bullets coming at me, I'll be running as fast as I can. Forget this walking business.'

At 4am Captain White, the lead officer of the impending attack moved amongst his men reassuring them that most of the Germans would be dead. They should walk to the German line and occupy their trenches in the name of Britain. He informed everyone that initially they would hear seventeen mines explode, finishing off any Germans who had survived the seven-day barrage.

At 7.30am precisely he would blow his whistle, their signal to climb the ladders and go over the top.

'Sounds like a plan' said Sam Turner.

'I hope he's bloody right,' muttered Frank.

They would soon find out. The time was 7am.

July 1st 1916

Crouching down in the trench Harry inspected his Enfield 303 and made sure the bayonet was fastened firmly. He couldn't quite imagine stabbing another human being with a bayonet, but would soon know if he could do it.

Time was ticking over very slowly. It seemed ages since the big guns stopped firing their deadly shells but in fact only five minutes had passed. At 7.05am the first of the explosions was heard and felt and then in quick succession another sixteen. The noise and booms knocked soldiers off their feet.

Their time to go over had arrived. Captain White blew his whistle and the first men climbed the ladders and began their walk across no man's land.

German machine guns cut them down.

> 'I thought the fucking Krauts were all supposed to be dead' Frank shouted.
>
> 'Never trust an officer' replied Sam.
>
> 'Don't blame them – it's the bloody General's fault.'
>
> 'All right you lot. Over you go and remember, walk, don't run. That's an order,' bellowed Captain White.

Sam was first, followed by Frank and finally a petrified Harry climbed the ladder to face the maelstrom.

Allied troops were being devastated by enemy fire because of the misconception that most German soldiers here had been eliminated by the seven-day barrage from the big guns or the seventeen mines that had just exploded under their trenches.

The Generals, particularly Haig, had underestimated how organised the Germans were. The Allies had not expected reinforced concrete dugouts that withstood fierce attacks. When the mines had finished exploding the Germans knew it was time to occupy their trenches. They simply carried their machine guns and positioned them ready to greet the British and her allies.

Harry saw Frank cut down by a shell explosion, bits and pieces flying everywhere. Keeping his head down Harry crawled across the muddy pockmarked ground, now littered with dead comrades. He fired many shots but had no idea if any of his bullets found their mark.

He heard an order to fall back to their own line and wasn't going to argue with a chance for his life, crawling as fast as he could back to relative safety.

Looking around his trench for a familiar face he didn't recognize anyone. Littering the space were dead soldiers who hadn't even made it over the top of the trenches.

Harry was shaking like a leaf. An officer poured rum into the surviving soldiers' tin cups to calm them down, Harry gulped his. He'd never tasted alcohol before, coughed and had another mouthful, enjoying the warmth he felt.

The first day of the Somme would go down in the annals as the blackest in British military history – 20,000 killed and 35,000 wounded.

Harry and his platoon were given relief for a few days despite the battle raging on around them and withdrew to the reserve line.

While Harry was in the reserve line he heard that his Father's regiment London 5th were stationed nearby and took the decision to leave the trench and walk the mile to where the 5th were positioned. It had been two years since he had seen his father and brothers and finding them was the very reason he enlisted in the first place.

When darkness swept over the valley he snuck out of the trench and began his quest. As he walked along the dirt road a motor vehicle approached flying a General's flag. The car pulled over and General Haig got out.

'Where do you think you're going Private?'

'Just enjoying the night air, Sir.'

'What Battalion are you with?'

'The 19th Sir.'

'You're a long way from your post Private. Are you sure you're not deserting, running away from your fellow soldiers who have put their lives on the line?'

'No Sir, as I said I'm simply taking a stroll.'

'I don't believe you. Hop into the front seat next to the driver. I'm taking you back to command headquarters.'

Harry did as instructed and the vehicle arrived at General Haig's headquarters at 10pm. After being locked in a cell with nothing but an iron bed and a bucket he didn't sleep at all that night. Around 9am an officer, Captain Needham, entered the cell and ordered Harry to follow him. They walked to an office where two other officers were seated.

'Private Jordan, are you aware just how much trouble you could be in?'

'Not really Sir, I was just going for a walk.'

'Were you? Was your commanding officer informed of your intentions?'

'No Sir, I didn't think it was necessary. I was only going for a short walk.'

'Soldier, you never leave your post whether in battle or not.'

'I won't do it again Sir.'

'No you won't. Are you aware of the penalty for leaving your post without permission?'

'No Sir.'

'Death by firing squad.'

'Oh my God, no' gasped Harry.

'So think hard about this question Private. Why did you leave your post without permission?'

Terrified, Harry explained how he'd hoped to find his father and brothers.

'What's your Father's full name and rank and what battalion is he attached to?'

Harry gave the requested information to the officer who promptly left the room while the other two stayed with Harry.

An hour later the Major returned with a grim look on his face.

'Private Jordan either everything you've told me is a lie or you're playing a very deadly game.'

'Sir, I've told you the truth, God's honour.'

'I can find no record of a Sergeant William Jordan.'

'I don't understand.'

'Neither do I. Return him back to his cell please Corporal Hay.'

Two days later Harry faced a court martial without legal representation. The court martial found him guilty of desertion and sentenced him to death by firing squad the following day.

Harry was led to the holding cell to contemplate what was ahead. A sergeant entered the cell at 9pm and gave Harry a mug of rum, which he took gratefully. The sergeant returned several times with more rum throughout the night. By the time morning came the sixteen-year-old boy was solidly drunk and unable to walk without assistance.

Two soldiers arrived at 7am, bound Harry with white cloth to restrain him before carrying him out to the courtyard where the execution would take place. They sat him down on a wooden chair as the same officer who had interrogated the young boy pinned a cloth over Harry's heart to provide a target for the firing squad.

Captain Needham ordered the firing squad to march into the courtyard and stand at attention. Once positioned, facing away from Harry, they would wait for the order to face the young boy and next, to fire.

Although drunk with the rum that had been given to him by his sympathetic gaolers, Harry was terrified.

Captain Needham gave the order to face the condemned soldier. Harry yelled out.

'Mother, Father.'

The officer ordered the squad to present arms, waited ten seconds and gave the order to fire.

Many of the shots hit the wall; deliberate misses; only two bullets wounded Harry. He was crying.

Needham unclipped his service revolver walked over to Harry and without a word shot him in the temple.

The body was taken for burial at the local cemetery. Harry became one of the 306 British soldiers executed for desertion or cowardice during the war. His name would not appear on any memorial honouring the war dead.

To Catch a Thief

Chapter 12

Lieutenant Colonel Oats had been informed by General Haig's office about Harry being executed for desertion but felt it would jeopardise the whole operation if he informed William at that stage.

William now had an idea why Captain Pittard had been killed but no solid proof. If he was to get a conviction he had to catch these bastards red handed.

Over the next few weeks he put a plan together, which although dangerous, should uncover the truth.

Major Albright, the alleged gang leader, was in fact his commanding officer. William knew he would end up in a lot of trouble if he accused Albright of the murder and it proved to be a false allegation. He could even be shot.

William's plan entailed waiting for the next medical shipment to come into the store. He and five trusted soldiers would hide in six large packing crates with peepholes allowing them to view the entire warehouse.

When the gang arrived to pilfer the drugs and replace the original manifests with the forged documents they would spring out of the crates and arrest the perpetrators.

William arranged for each soldier to carry a Lee Enfield 303 plus one Lewis machine gun operated by the gunner in the end crate. He wasn't leaving anything to chance.

The storehouse was manned from 7am to 7pm giving the gang a twelve-hour time frame to enter the store and steal the drugs. It also meant that William and his men might be stuck in their storage crates for a bloody long time.

Captain Sykes and his band of men entered the building soon after closing time and took position in their individual crates. Each man had food rations and a water bottle. Not exactly luxury but it would keep them going for the duration.

Nobody could communicate with each other so it was essential that each soldier knew the plan inside out. They couldn't leave their hiding spot so relieving themselves was also confined to the crate.

At 3am the large entrance doors were rolled open and an army truck reversed in, two men were in the vehicle and two more walked beside it.

The gang approached the newly arrived medical supplies and prised open the tops with crowbars. Major Albright stood back holding the two versions of the manifest; it was critical that the numbers were correct.

Once William saw them loading the supplies into the truck he lifted the top of his crate, as did the other five soldiers. Pointing their weapons at the startled thieves, William shouted 'Halt! Drop your weapons or we'll shoot.'

The gang knew they were outgunned and did as they were ordered. William approached his commanding officer and took the documentation he was holding then handcuffed the Major.

'I am arresting you all on suspicion of murder and stealing government goods.'

Sergeant Abbott, Corporal Bennet, and an unknown Private were also handcuffed. William and his men arranged for transport to ferry the prisoners to the barracks for incarceration until a court martial could be arranged.

William invited his team back to the cottage for a celebratory scotch. It had been a long night, albeit successful. After everyone departed William tried to get a few hours sleep before he contacted Lieutenant Colonel Oats with the good news.

'Hello Sir, it's Captain Jordan.'

'You mean Captain Sykes don't you?'

'No sir I've cracked the case. I think I should start going by my real name.'

'Cracked the case; good man.'

William went through the scenario and named the alleged perpetrators.

Lieutenant Colonel Oats was astounded as he knew Major Albright very well, or so he thought.

A court martial was arranged the following week with the four accused represented by a Major Thomas, barrister-at-law.

It didn't matter how good the defence was, it was a watertight case, a guilty verdict pronounced and four death sentences.

The executions by firing squad took place in the same courtyard where young Harry Jordan had met his maker.

Shortly after the trial ended William was notified of his son's death; to say he was devastated was an understatement.

Lieutenant Colonel Oats arranged three weeks leave for William, Henry, and Sam to return to England and try to recover from their ordeal.

When William wrote to Victoria he had trouble finding the right words.

He simply wrote:

My Darling Victoria,

I am alive and well and will be returning to England shortly to spend some time with you and the family.

Your loving Husband

William

When Victoria, learned of William's mission and the deception she was furious but after a few days accepted it was one of the many sacrifices made during this terrible war.

William returned to the front as a Captain, taking part in a number of battles including Passchendaele. He survived the war and returned to England and the police force.

Henry and Sam also survived the war going home as Corporals.

William committed himself to clear the name of his son Harry.

Baby Boy Warrior

Chapter 13

The young Serbian boy was playing outside his house in the pretty village of Trbusnica in Serbia. He was doing what most eight year old boys did while the horrendous battles of World War One were taking place – playing war.

His Mother, Father, three sisters and four brothers were inside the house preparing for the midday meal. They were a large and happy family who all worked on the family's dairy farm under the shadow of Gucevo, the largest mountain in that part of Serbia. They weren't wealthy but the farm income was enough to keep them clothed and fed.

They all knew this was going to come to an end; the Austrian Hungarians had declared war on Serbia as a result of Archduke Franz Ferdinand of Austria and his wife, Sophie being killed by a Serbian nationalist group, the 'Black Hand', in Sarajevo. Austria-Hungary's declaration of war on Serbia was effectively the beginning of the First World War.

The two eldest boys were intending to enlist the very next day. This would break up the family but was a decision supported by both their parents, Drazen and Ivanka.

Bosco, the eldest boy, outside to pick some vegetables for the roast dinner, heard raucous laughter and obscene language emanating from the front of the farmhouse. Sneaking around the side of the house to see who these men were he poked his head around a corner but one of the Austrian soldiers spotted him, raised a rifle and shot Bosco through the head. The young man fell; another soldier approached him and fired another shot, just to be sure.

The rest of the family heard the shots and raced outside only to be slaughtered where they stood. Apart from the eight-year old boy the entire family was eliminated in five minutes. Terrified, young Davor saw the whole thing and ran as fast as he could through the forest heading for Gucevo the mountain he hoped would protect him.

He hid in a small crevasse between two large rocks, shaking and trying not to cry in case the drunken soldiers heard him. Eventually, cold and hungry, he decided to leave his safe haven and try to find some food. While walking along a mountain path he came across Major Stevan Tucovic.

> 'Hey, what's a young boy doing up here all alone? What's your name boy?'
>
> 'Davor, Sir.'
>
> 'What are you doing here? Where are your parents?'
>
> 'The soldiers shot them.'
>
> 'What soldiers?'
>
> 'I don't know but I think they were Austrians. They shot my brothers and sisters too.'
>
> 'Where do you live son?'
>
> 'I can show you.'
>
> 'OK, you lead the way. By the way what is your name again?'
>
> 'Davor.'

'Right Davor, you show us the way.'

Major Tucovic and his men followed the young boy until they reached the farmhouse with nine bodies lying outside and inside the house ransacked.

Major Tucovic ordered his men to dig graves where they placed the bodies and covered them. Davor watched and cried.

'Well. I am at a loss what to do with you Davor. Any suggestions?'

'I want to come with you. I want to join the army and kill Austrians.'

'Do you now. Can you throw a grenade?'

'I know how to throw rocks.'

The major unclipped a grenade from his belt instructed the eight year old how to pull the pin and hurl the explosive. Davor completed the exercise faultlessly.

'OK soldier, so you would like to kill the Austrians that shot your family?'

'Yes Sir.'

'Men, can I have two volunteers to accompany young Davor as he avenges the death of his family?'

All twenty soldiers raised their hands, the Major chose his best men. The three soldiers moved down the valley until they reached the next farmhouse and sure enough, could hear laughter and drunken cursing

Moving slowly towards the murderous Austrians they got within range and Private Mišović threw the first grenade, which exploded in the middle of the group. Davor threw the second. The plundering soldiers were all killed.

Davor became a fighter of the Serbian army and an adopted child of the sixth artillery regiment of the Drina division. Major Tucovic ordered his soldiers to let Davor fire the cannon three times a day, so he could continue to avenge the deaths of his family.

At the beginning of the war the Austrian attacks were pushed back as the Serbs made some gains, however the Germans reinforced the Austrian attacks with fresh divisions adding to the Serb's problems. Bulgaria joined forces with the Germans while the poorly equipped and exhausted Serbian troops faced destruction and decided to retreat. In an act of sheer desperation the entire Serbian army gathered equipment and civilians, withdrawing to Greece via Albania.

During this long and epic journey Private Mišović took the young Davor under his wing. They were now brothers in arms. One night while warming up next to a fire, Mišović, losing his strength through lack of food, said to Davor 'Son, I'm afraid I won't be able to move on much further… If I fall, promise to just walk on'.

Hunger and the freezing winter eventually broke the strong man who stumbled and fell in the snow. Davor stopped and gave Mišović his hand.

'No, keep going, Davor. Please.'

Davor sat down by his side and curled up, 'Sir, I won't go any further... I will die here with you.'

Hearing the boy's words Mišović gathered what was left of his strength and resolve, stood up, and started moving again. Somehow they managed the last 10km and arrived at the Corfu dockyard.

Later on in Corfu young Davor was given a star on each of his shoulders... And so the nine-year-old Davor Gavrić became the youngest corporal ever to be commissioned in history. Davor had walked with the regiment through the whole of Serbia and Albania enduring more on that journey to Corfu than many adults.

Le plus jeune soldat serbe agé de 12 ans en action a Belgrade.

Later he took part in breaking the front of Thessalonica, which decided the outcome of the Serbian-Austrian war. In battle he was shot and wounded. He was promoted to sub-sergeant.

After the war Davor travelled to England where he finished his schooling, returning to Belgrade in 1921 where he lived until his death in 1993.

ANZAC

Infant ry

Chapter 14

Australia and New Zealand were among the first Commonwealth countries to declare allegiance to their mother country, Britain, when the First World War broke out.

What inspired these young men to cross oceans and travel halfway across the world away to fight in a conflict not of their making nor threatening their own security?

Australia and New Zealand felt more like Britain than a part of Oceania, and accordingly loyalties lay with their King, in a country far away. In schoolrooms and in their own homes, boys and girls were raised to feel a strong sense of loyalty and obligation to Britain where many of their parents and grandparents were born.

It is therefore understandable that boys as young as twelve ran off to fight the war, not really understanding what they were getting into.

Private Cecil Thomas of Manly, Sydney, enlisted at fourteen and was transported with thousands of other troops to Egypt to undertake additional training.

On March 6, 1916, Private Thomas was 'taken on strength' into the 45th Battalion, transferring to the 13th Battalion later that month. He boarded a troopship to Marseilles in June 1916, transported to the Western front where the war was raging. In the second half of 1916 he took part in the horrendous battles at Mouquet Farm and Pozieres where Australian forces suffered 6,300 casualties.

Fortunately Private Thomas wasn't one of them. He shipped home to Sydney, a veteran of war at 16 years of age.

Leonard Pickering came from a good family who owned and operated a large greengrocer in Neutral Bay, a beautiful leafy suburb in northern Sydney.

Leonard was near completing his schooling at Neutral Bay Public School where he generally came in the top ten per cent of his class.

He was also a keen rugby player in the winter and cricket player in the summer.

All in all, life was good for young Leonard at thirteen years of age. Then, Australia declared war on Germany, Austria, and Turkey, supporting Britain in what would be a long and protracted war.

Leonard read all that he could on what was happening in Europe during the first year of the war. He skipped classes to attend recruitment rallies and while at one of these rallies he made a monumental decision to change his name and age and enlist.

He chose the name Richard Matheson, informing the recruitment officer he was an eighteen-year-old orphan. On August 6th 1915, he was accepted.

One of the reasons Leonard was so keen to enlist was the fact that his two older brothers, Harry and Dudley, had joined up earlier the same year.

Leonard's father, Joseph, arrived home from the shop at the usual time of 6pm, poured himself a beer and his wife Annabelle a sherry. They sat out on the back veranda, which had a view of Sydney Harbour where they could see yachts coming in after an afternoon's sail.

'So, how was your day dear?' asked Annabelle.

'Pretty good, although takings were slightly down but I'm sure we'll make them up by the end of the week. How about you, what did you do today?'

'The usual, two loads of washing and a basket full of ironing. Mary Hall dropped in to see me, the poor thing's all upset about her two boys enlisting. She's very concerned she won't see them again.'

'They'll be all right. They're fine strapping lads just like our three boys.'

'I hope you're right Joe if anything happened to Harry or Dudley I'm sure I wouldn't cope. At least we have Leonard home safe with us.'

'They'll look out for each other, that's what we did when I fought in the Sudan. Where's young Leonard?'

'I haven't seen him this afternoon but I assume he'll be home soon or miss out on dinner. It's his favourite; meatloaf and veges.'

Dinner came and went with out any sign of Leonard, his parents became quite concerned when he had still not got home by eight. Joseph decided to visit the local police station in case his son had been in an accident.

'Hello officer, my name is Joseph Pickering I'm concerned for the welfare of my son Leonard.'

'Why's that?'

'He's missing? He is always home for dinner at 6.30pm but he hasn't arrived as yet.'

'It's a bit early to start a search of any kind, I think you should wait until tomorrow morning. If he hasn't shown up by then we'll see what we can do. You don't think he's run away to join the army do you?'

'Hardly, he's only thirteen years old.'

'Yes well that is a bit young isn't it?'

Joe left the police station with out any sense of satisfaction whatsoever. He walked the mile back to his house pondering the various alternatives. Could Leo have enlisted? He could have lied about his age. No, surely not, he was just a boy, the army wouldn't accept him.

It was a sleepless night, either Annabelle or Joseph getting up every hour to check if Leonard had snuck back into his room.

The next morning Joseph returned to the police station and reported his son still missing. The duty officer requested a photo to display on their missing persons board. Joseph knew that wasn't going to achieve much but agreed to drop one in later that day. He also decided to visit the recruitment centre at the Paddington Barracks, catching the ferry across to Circular Quay and then a taxi to the barracks.

Joseph entered the wide doors to find a queue of expectant young men answering the call. Standing out as the old man in the crowd an officer approached him, enquiring about his intentions. Joseph explained that he feared his thirteen-year-old boy had lied about his age and enlisted.

> 'I can't believe we would have accepted such a young lad although it's hard to pick their age these days. Follow me sir and we'll check the enlistment register.'

Joe followed the officer into an office with a dozen or so army personnel going over recruitment papers and such.

> 'Now, what's your boy's name Mr…?'

> 'Pickering, Joseph Pickering.'

> 'What's your son's Christian name?'

> 'Leonard.'

> 'Right, let's see if we can find him, they're listed in alphabetical order so it shouldn't be too difficult.'

After about fifteen minutes of checking and rechecking no Leonard Pickering could be found listed in the documents.

> 'Well Mr Pickering it doesn't look like your boy registered here but you could try some of the smaller recruitment offices.'

> 'Where would they be?'

'Mainly areas such as Parramatta and Newcastle.'

'I don't think he would have enlisted there as he had no way of getting to either place. Thank you anyway officer.'

Joseph was beginning to get really worried that something untoward had happened to his son.

It was a very quiet subdued dinner that night just Joe and Annabelle with their older boys in training camp about ready to ship to Egypt.

Victoria Barracks Paddington Sydney

7th August 1915

Private Richard Matheson aka Leonard Pickering woke on his first morning in barracks to a bugler sounding Reveille. He washed and donned his new khaki uniform then headed to breakfast in the mess hall. It felt quite intimidating to sit down at a table with so many men between 18-40 years of age.

After breakfast they were ordered onto the parade ground for their first session in how to march properly. Richard aka Leonard wasn't sure how marching was going to save his life when he got to the front but obviously the officers in charge felt marching was a significant defence mechanism because that's all they did in the first two weeks of basic training.

Richard had got to know a few men in his barracks, they all seemed to be pretty young although he knew no one was as young as he was. He wrote a letter to his parents explaining why he had enlisted and assured them he would be fine, expressing the desire to find his two brothers once he landed in France.

Upon receiving the letter Joe and Annabelle, although concerned for the welfare of their youngest son, were at the same time relieved he was well and hadn't fallen victim to unsavoury elements.

Joseph knew that life in an army at war was not easy, having experienced it himself in the Sudan. Feeling the need to keep an eye on Leonard Joseph decided to enlist. Initially Annabelle was horrified by the fact that the four men in her life would be fighting in a war halfway around the world. It would be she who had to manage the shop and keep things going on the home front. Eventually she came around to Joe's line of thinking and understood his intention.

Joe made his way to Victoria Barracks, he too lied about his age writing down that he was 44 as opposed to his real age of 52.

He passed the physical and was accepted into the AIF.

By the time Joseph had settled into army life, Leonard or Richard as he was now known, had passed training and was sailing to Egypt.

After breezing through the eight-week basic training Joseph was soon on his way to Egypt, along with 2,000 other recent recruits.

Father and Son

Chapter 15

Richard aka Leonard, was stationed in the Australian camp of Mena, a huge tent city very close to the pyramids which he found astounding, not to mention the Great Sphinx and of course Cairo.

Mena Camp Egypt

Mena Camp. Photo taken from the Great Pyramid

He had ventured into Cairo a couple of times with his mates; he was soon to turn fourteen so he felt he was almost a man. The narrow streets crowded with stalls, merchants selling genuine artefacts from the tombs of the pharaohs and the painted ladies offering pleasure and invariably pain, all painted a picture he had never dreamed of back home.

Richard was lying on a stretcher bed in his six-man tent when one of his mates came in.

'Hey Rich there's an old bloke outside who reckons he knows you.'

'Yeah, what's his name?'

Joseph walked into the tent.

'His name's Father to you but you can call me Papa.'

Richard sprang off the stretcher and looked at his father in disbelief.

'Papa it really is you.'

The two soldiers hugged each other. Richard wouldn't let go until Joe suggested they go for a walk outside.

The two men walked towards the pyramids. Joseph had always wanted to see them since he was a boy in school.

'So Papa, I don't understand what you're doing here and how did you find me? I changed my name so that I couldn't be found.'

'I did some clever detective work, having a recent photograph helped.'

'I still don't understand what you're doing here.'

'I just wanted to be near Harry and Dud and fight for my country.'

'They're noble causes son but for God's sake you're only thirteen. You asked me why I'm here well I came over to keep an eye on you just to make sure you're all right.'

'I'm glad you're here Papa. By the way I turned fourteen a few weeks ago.'

'I think you better start calling me Joseph we don't want to raise any suspicions do we?'

'Ok. Joseph, have you heard where Harry and Dud are at the moment?'

'Your Mother and I received a letter before I departed Australia. It appears both of them are stationed in a place called Ypres in Flanders. I don't know too much more but by all accounts it's a pretty dangerous place.

Joe was right; the Ypres was under constant German shell attack. There were a number of key villages near Ypres and both the British and the Germans regarded them as crucial to hold and occupy.

One of those villages was Pozieres and that was where Harry and Dudley were heading with the 1st Australian division.

Ypres Flanders 1916

AIF Marching Through Ypres 1916

Ypres 1912

The attack on Pozieres was launched on 23 July 1916; this was to become known as the Battle of Pozieres Ridge. Australian and British forces fought hard for an area that comprised a relatively high observation post over the surrounding countryside. An additional benefit of securing this area was the alternative rear approach to the Thiepval defences where the Germans were entrenched.

Primarily, the Australian 1st Division were given the task of capturing Pozieres Ridge. This had been an objective for capture since the first day of the Somme offensive. The Australians succeeded in capturing the ridge by August 4. Having launched their own offensive almost two weeks earlier, the British 48th Division assisted them in the attack.

The Australian diggers succeeded in capturing Pozieres village itself, after which they moved across the main road towards Gibraltar, a German strongpoint. A mere two hundred yards separated the Australians from the attack's main objective, Pozieres Ridge, heavily defended by the securely entrenched German troops. Two lines of trenches needed to be overcome before the ridge could be claimed, although this action created a heavy toll on the Australian and British troops.

Later on that first day, July 23, the British 17th Warwickshire Regiment joined the Australians to the northwest of Pozieres village. The Germans weren't going anywhere; they defended the ridge valiantly.

The 2nd Australian Division subsequently relieved their comrades and continued the attack on the ridge for a further four days before they too were relieved. Allied casualties at this stage were running at a costly 3,500.

The ridge finally fell on August 4 after almost two weeks of bitter fighting. However, both Mouquet Farm and Thiepval remained under German control. General Gough, the British commander, insisted they take these two targets and persisted with this plan, resulting in 23,000 Australian casualties. Gough came under Australian criticism for his persistence in pushing the advance over five weeks. Scepticism of the quality of British leadership had already intensified following the notable failure of an earlier Battle at Fromelles, west of Lille, on July 19-20 by the Australian 5th Division, intended to divert German attention away from the Somme. During this battle, the Australians suffered 5,708 casualties, of which a total of 4,000 were fatalities; a further 400 were captured and marched by the Germans through Lille. Their lives as prisoners of war were about to begin.

The Rock

Chapter 16

Harry Pickering was exhausted and fed up with what seemed to be futile battles and horrendous casualties. He and his younger brother, Dudley, had signed up to fight for King and country but he didn't feel like they were doing that, it seemed like they were fighting for bloody incompetent British Generals like Gough and Haig.

General Haig

General Gough

July 23rd 1916 Pozieres

Harry and his brother Dud together with the remains of their platoon were all waiting for the order to advance.

The sound of the British artillery barrage was deafening and relentless.

> 'Fucking hell boys, how in the name of God could the Boche bastards survive this?' said Ernie Parsons.

'Fucked if I know Ernie, what I do know is they'll give it back to us twice as hard when they get the opportunity,' responded Harry.

'Yeah you're right there Harry.'

'Right cobbers we've got to try and stick together and look out for each other. Ok?' George Duke the platoon leader said.

'Don't worry about us George we'll be all right,' said Dud.

'Do you hear anything mate?'

'No it's all gone quiet.'

'You know what that means don't you?'

'I'm afraid I do, we could be about to die.'

'Come on Dud, we're the Pickerings.'

They heard the order being passed along their line in whispered tones.

'We go at 3am exactly.'

Harry looked at his watch. It was 2.55am, just enough time to jot a quick note to his parents back home.

Dear Mum and Dad

Dudley and I are just about to confront the enemy but don't worry I know we'll be fine. We're in a place called Pozieres. I'm sure it was a pretty little village once but now it's just rubble. There isn't a single tree or flower to be seen.

Dud's holding up well and we both keep an eye out for one another, it seems to have worked so far.

Say hello to Leonard from us both.

Your loving son

Harry

Harry folded the note and placed it in his top pocket. He would post it after the battle.

At 3am the signal was given and the Australians began running for the German trenches. The familiar sound of German Maxim machine guns ripping through Australian flesh was heard along with screaming and the guttural noise of men choking on their own blood.

Harry and Dud were able to penetrate the German trenches where they discovered two of the enemy waiting to greet them. Harry thrust his bayonet into the soldier opposing him before the German could get off a shot. He turned to see Dudley just standing there with a dazed look on his face.

> 'What's wrong with you mate? Come on we've got a job to do, there's plenty more where these bastards came from.'

Dudley didn't say a thing he just looked at his brother and fell to his knees and then collapsed into the trench. A bayonet thrust had mortally wounded Dudley, but he had been able to kill the Kraut before dying himself.

Harry was horrified but he couldn't stop to grieve, he had to keep moving through the trench shooting any Germans he could find. He was in a killing frenzy seeking revenge for his fallen brother.

The first battalion were successful in capturing the Pozieres trench that ringed the village to the south. Mission accomplished but at what cost?

It was established by the officers that stage one of the battle had been completed successfully with the German trench captured by the Australians and the British. Thousands had died achieving this objective.

The 1st and 3rd ANZAC Battalion then moved on Pozieres village, or what was left of it. They reached the Albert-Bapaume road, secured that location, and moved into the ruins of the village. Although pleased with their progress command knew taking the next objective was going to be difficult, certainly no picnic to reach their target, Gibraltar.

Pozieres Before the Attack

Pozieres After the Attack

Harry and a Few Mates at Pozieres

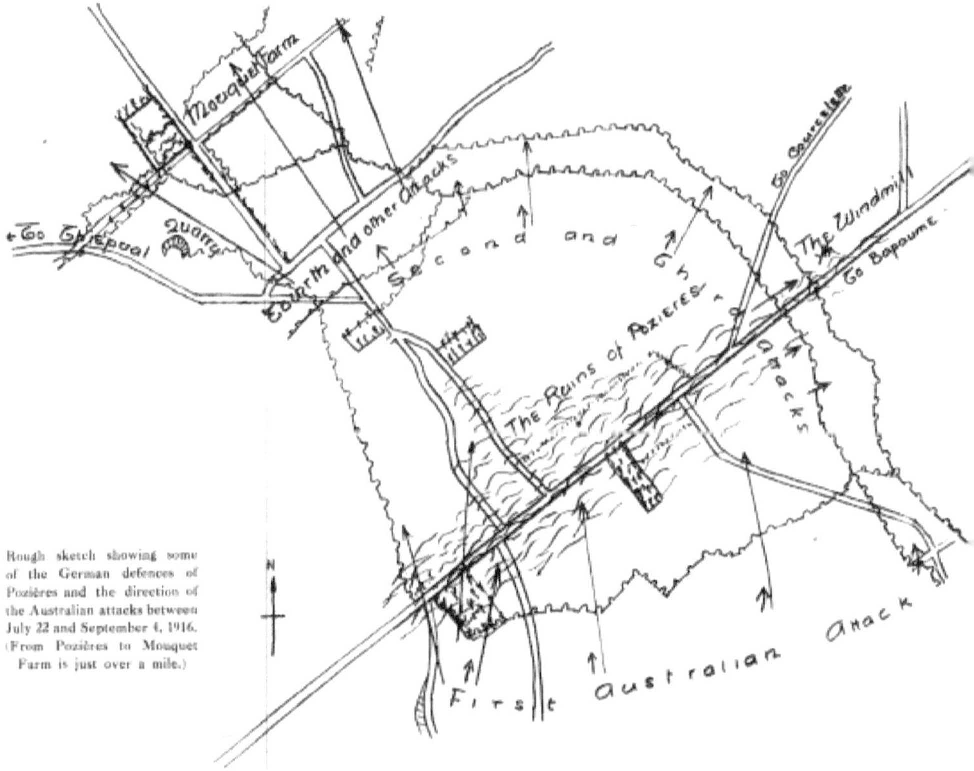

Rough sketch showing some of the German defences of Pozières and the direction of the Australian attacks between July 22 and September 4, 1916. (From Pozières to Mouquet Farm is just over a mile.)

Mud Map of Pozieres

There were minimal survivors from the German garrison and those left retreated to the northern edge of the village. Although the Australian's intention was to capture the old German lines as far as the road, unfortunately they failed, partly due to strong resistance from the German defenders occupying deep dugouts and machine gun nests and partly due to the confusion of a night attack on featureless terrain.

Weeks of bombardment had reduced the ridge to a field of craters and it was virtually impossible to distinguish where trench lines had run. The failure to take these old German lines left the eastern end of Pozieres vulnerable so the Australians formed a flank, somewhat short of their objective.

Two officers, Major John Jeffries and Captain Bruce Menzies, were sitting amongst the burnt-out ruins after the first day of fighting at Pozieres discussing the best way to attack Gibraltar.

The scene could have come from Dante's *Inferno* – blackened trees, dead bodies strewn around, moaning and troubled breathing in the background. Stretcher-bearers were running everywhere attempting to save the wounded.

Their men had done a magnificent job in capturing Pozieres against the odds. What they achieved would be the envy of the British in their campaign at the Somme.

The two Australian officers noticed a British messenger running along Dead Man's Road jumping over bodies and fallen trees, obviously an important message was to be delivered.

He reached the officers, handed them the envelope then slumped on the ground exhausted. Major Jeffries read the message shook his head and read it out aloud to his comrade.

> *'Lately, there have been a number of cases where men have failed to salute an army commander passing in his car, despite the car carrying his flag upon the bonnet. This practice must cease.'*

Signed General Gough

'Where's his fucking priorities? The man's a lunatic!' complained Captain Menzies.

'I couldn't agree more. But, getting back to Gibraltar. First he denies us the support we need with an artillery barrage because his reports show there are no Germans on the north side which, judging from the constant sniper fire is bullshit. Now, just as we are about to attack the biggest and ugliest German fortification for miles, he tells us to make sure our boys salute the pompous bastard as he drives past in his Rolls fucking Royce.'

'Bruce don't worry about him. The reality is he's our commander and we're obliged to obey. If our diggers refuse to salute well, so be it. Now, I think we have the plan of attack worked out. Let's go and take the bitch and kill a few Germans.'

'Yes Sir.'

The 1st and 3rd Battalions attacked and took Gibraltar early that day capturing 23 prisoners.

The elation was short-lived as British artillery started blasting K-Trench, which was quite close to Gibraltar, requiring the Australians to vacate the premises.

They came back in the afternoon and captured it yet again.

The Remains of Gibraltar

Harry was exhausted and grief-stricken, he had lost his brother, his best mate. Why had he survived the carnage and poor Dudley had not? He would gladly have traded places.

Their Mother received the telegram two weeks after Dudley's death and his father received it at the same time. Since early 1916, Joe and Leonard had been in the 55th Infantry Battalion; they were now in Ypres awaiting orders that would take them into the next battle.

Richard aka Leonard stepped into his father's tent to find him sobbing on his stretcher.

'Papa, I mean Joseph, what's the matter?'

Joseph didn't respond, crying uncontrollably, his whole body shaking.

'Joseph tell me what's wrong.'

Finally after several minutes Joseph passed the piece of paper he had been grasping.

It is with deep regret that I have to inform you that your son Private Dudley Pickering No 129765 was killed in action at Pozieres on July 23rd 1916

Signed

Lieutenant Colonel Edward Smith

'No, oh my God, no, not Dudley. It must be a mistake.'

Leonard dropped to his knees and began crying, now Joseph's turn to try and console his son.

Eventually both Pickering men had calmed down to the point of talking to each other.

They hoped Harry would be able to tell them how it happened, whenever it was they saw him next. Neither soldier slept much that night; at about 3am Joe made a decision to go to his commanding officer in the morning, confess his true age and that of Leonard. He hoped the right thing would be done and they would be shipped back home.

When the Commander heard Joseph and Leonard's story he agreed to discharge them both. In March 1917, Father and son returned to Australia aboard HMAT *Ulysses*.

Wild Rivers

Chapter 17

1914

Malcolm McTaggart was a strong strapping lad who looked and behaved much older than his 13 years. His mother, Martha, thought it was because he had lost his father when he was only five. The family ran a paddle steamer, the *Murray Princess,* along the mighty Murray River. The family consisted of three boys and two girls; Malcolm was the youngest and Ron, at 23, the eldest. The middle boy, Alex, was 20 years old. The two girls were Anna, 17, and at 19, Jane.

The paddle steamer plied its way from Echuca, where the family lived, berthing at docks along the rivers Murray and Darling.

September 1914

Alex arrived home with some exciting news; he had enlisted in the Army. While picking up some supplies for the next steamer voyage he came across a recruitment drive in the main street of town. Six men of the Light Horse brigade riding on magnificent steeds with an Army band following. Alex caught up in the fervour of it all signed up.

The Murray Princess

'Mate I know you think you're doing the right thing but it leaves us short on the *Murray Princess*' said Ron.

'I know Ron, but I'm sure Malcolm and the girls will make up for me. It's important to fight for your King and country, don't you think?'

'It's hard for me to say, but no, things haven't been easy for me of late. I've received half a dozen white feathers so far, sent anonymously in the mail. I would dearly love to join up but it would be impossible particularly now that you've enlisted. I have to keep the *Princess* and the family going.'

'I didn't know you were getting white feathers mate, that's so wrong. Who do these anonymous bastards think they are? At least they could call you a coward to your face then you could defend your actions.'

'It doesn't matter. The key issue is I'm staying home and you're going over there to fight. At least you'll know I'm here looking after things so when you return you can take up where you left. I should have a shoebox full of feathers by the time you arrive back home.'

'Have you told mum and the girls yet?' asked Ron.

'No I thought I'd tell you and Malcolm first. I'll bring it up over dinner tonight.'

Malcolm hadn't said a word throughout the conversation, he just sat on a hay bale and took it all in. Neither of his brothers asked his opinion.

When Alex announced his decision at the table there was a mixture of shock and excitement from his sisters and quiet contemplation from Martha, his mother. She knew the pain of losing a loved one; her much-loved husband had drowned in the very river that had been his lifeblood. Martha also knew the heartache she would feel if her son Alex did not return from this war.

Malcolm continued working on the *Murray Princess* for several months after Alex had departed for foreign shores, but never stopped thinking about enlisting although conscious of the fact that if he did leave, his older brother and his sisters would be running the business a man short.

1916

Malcolm was hoping the Government would win the conscription referendum, then there would be no argument, he would be obliged to go and fight for his country. There was the question of his age but he knew of other boys in the area lying about their ages.

The actual conscription debate began in 1916 when Prime Minister Billy Hughes visited the war front. On his return to Australia the PM advocated his support for conscription as there was no doubt Australia needed more soldiers. In 1916 and again in 1917 a referendum was held. Three states voted Yes and three No. The majority of the population was against the amendment to the original law and both referendums failed.

As a result, the need for recruitment was stronger than ever and intensified campaigns were popping up in every city. Some of the arguments against conscription were that enough lives had been lost and that farmers need more men to work the land for food. There were two things needed for the war more than anything: men and money.

Malcolm made his decision, and ran away from home to fight in the war.

He joined the band of brothers on the recruitment train bound for Broadmeadows training camp. The camp consisted of tents, and mud, and more mud; it was a boggy quagmire. Many of the recruits became ill with complaints such as gastroenteritis, possibly a good training program for the conditions they were about to face.

After eight weeks of basic training the enthusiastic recruits were transported to Melbourne where they were loaded onto the troop ship *Ascanius* and sailed to Egypt on the 10th November 1915.

Ascanius **Departs From Port Melbourne**

After eight weeks of high seas, cramped conditions and seasickness, Malcolm arrived in Cairo, Egypt. There were some upsides from the sea voyage, meeting a couple of blokes who became good mates and learning how to play two-up.

Frank Johnson and Peter Nye became Malcolm's best mates; they were both 20 and took the young pup under their protective wing.

Apart from climbing the Great Pyramid and playing desert cricket, their time at Mena Camp was taken up by training. None of the Aussies could see any benefit from marching in full-pack across the desert sand in searing heat. They were all quite sure Northern France and Belgium had somewhat different terrain and climate.

March 1916

Malcolm was placed into the 2nd Anzac Corps, 5th Division. General Godley was his Commanding Officer.

March 19th 1916

Troopships carrying the Australian 1st and 2nd Divisions arrive in Marseilles in the south of France.

There wasn't much time for sightseeing in Marseilles, no sooner had they landed when they were loaded onto a train heading for French Flanders.

Without enough room on the train for games of two-up instead the diggers played cards and looked at the scenery as it went past.

Mal and his mates, together with the other Australian troops, were billeted in the St Omer-Hazebrouke region of French Flanders. This was commonly known as the nursery because the majority of soldiers were young and inexperienced.

April 1916

Finally the Australians began to see some action with the 2nd and 1st Divisions taking up positions on the front line.

Meanwhile Malcolm impatiently waited for the 5th Division to be called up for battle and in July 1916 heard Fromelles was their objective.

The Battle of Fromelles

The Battle of Fromelles began on July 19th 1916 and concluded on the following day. The battle plan attempted to deter the Germans from moving resources away from Fromelles to reinforce their troops fighting in the Battle of the Somme fifty miles to the south.

The area around Fromelles was seen as a 'quiet' sector allowing the Germans to move their troops around relatively easily. The battle plan was an attempt to disrupt these troop movements while putting pressure on the German High Command. The overall objective of General Haig was to force the Germans to deplete their force at the Somme by reinforcing their troops engaged in battle at Fromelles.

On July 19th Australian and British troops from two divisions (and the 5th Australian Division and 61st Division) attacked German positions at Fromelles. The German lines had been shelled for seven hours by 200,000 artillery rounds.

Much to the German's astonishment, British military intelligence had failed to discover the original trench lines had been abandoned some time before. New, considerably more sophisticated trenches had been constructed with gun emplacements made of reinforced concrete and deep bunkers where the German troops could wait during bombardments then reappear with machine guns at-the-ready to greet their Allied adversaries.

When the seven hours of bombardment ceased a deathly silence followed indicating to the Germans that the Allies were about to launch their infantry attack.

When the Allies attacked they were hit by a German artillery bombardment that left many dead in their own trenches. Those troops who succeeded in climbing over the parapet faced ferocious machine gun fire decimating the attacking troops. The British troops, the 61st was badly hit, they were forced to retire to their own lines after suffering heavy casualties. The Australian 5th were more successful reaching what military intelligence thought were the German front lines, only to find them abandoned and flooded. The actual German lines were 200 metres further on and heavily defended. By July 20th they, like the 61st had to retreat after suffering very high casualties.

This attack, a complete disaster due to incompetent generals acting on incorrect intelligence, resulted in the greatest Australian loss of troops during a single day of any war – 5,533 in total. The magnitude of this figure is still valid despite the wars Australia has participated in throughout the 20th and 21st centuries. Casualties including those killed, wounded, and missing, accounted for about 90% of the Australians involved and another 1,547 British troops, about 50% of those involved. If the British 61st had not retreated to their lines they would have suffered a similar casualty rate as the Australians.

At one stage, many Australian men lay wounded in no man's land. A temporary truce was planned for collecting the wounded but the British High Command vetoed this suggestion. How many more deaths were caused by this cruel decision?

Fromelles was one of the worst disasters to befall the Australian Army in the whole of World War One, souring relations between British and Australian senior army commanders.

Preparing to Go Over the Top – Fromelles

Mal, Frank and Peter had been waiting in a damp, stinking, rat-infested trench for what seemed like hours listening to the never-ending bombardment of the British big guns. Mal's ears were aching from the incessant blasts but no complaints if the shells killed most of the Krauts.

'Hey Pup, how are you going mate?' asked Peter.

'Yeah all right, I can't wait for these guns to stop though.'

'Don't be too impatient mate. When those fuckers stop firing it's time for us poor buggers to go over the top.'

'It might be nice to get out of this stinking trench and go for a run.'

'Yeah right,' muttered Frank.

Their commanding officer, Brigadier General 'Pompey' Elliott, was moving down the trench giving his men words of encouragement. Pompey opposed this attack and had tried to convince the British command it was futile and overly dangerous. They hadn't listened.

'Frank, it's all gone quiet,' said Mal.

'Yes mate, check your bayonet. It's time for that run,' said Peter.

Captain Green looked at his watch – now 5.25am.

'Men we've got five minutes until we go over the top. Just enough time for one last check of your equipment and a quick prayer.

At 5.30am Captain Green blew his whistle. The men of the 59th Battalion, Australian 5th Division began to clamber up the ladder, the first men were immediately shot and fell back into the trenches.

Less keen to climb the ladder now Mal nevertheless knew he had to go and go immediately. He climbed the ladder to face the hail of machine gun bullets, Frank and Peter close behind him.

Mal ran as fast as he could, only another 400 yards to go before he had the chance to kill some Germans. Jumping inside a large shell crater he found some Australians occupying the space, most obviously dead but one still alive. Mal asked if he was OK, receiving a guttural reply.

'Shoot me, please someone shoot me.'

Moving closer Mal could see blood all over the front of the digger's uniform. He gently unbuttoned the coat and the man's guts just fell out. Mal was aghast. Never in all his life… Aiming his 303 rifle at the poor bastard's head, Mal shot him between the eyes.

Suddenly aware he had spent too much time in the crater Mal climbed the embankment and peered out to a scene of unmitigated carnage. Crouching as low as possible he ran towards the enemy line firing the odd shot but knowing full well he probably hadn't hit anything or anyone. It wasn't possible to see Peter or Frank but the thick smoke made it unlikely he would easily identify anyone.

To Mal's amazement he arrived at the first German trench. Unfortunately there was no one home – the real defensive line was still another 200 yards on. He looked around for an officer to get some direction but all the men nearby were privates like him.

It was decided to stay put until nightfall before returning to their own line for another full-strength charge at the Germans.

Early the next morning the remaining Australians were still holed up in the disused German trench. There had been no opportunity for them to retreat.

Mal was dozing when a loud voice woke him. He looked up to see several German soldiers standing along the parapet, rifles pointed at the bedraggled Australian diggers, and although none of them spoke German it was clear they were being ordered out of the trench.

Mal and his newfound mates clambered out with their hands up and weapons left behind. Twenty in all, they were marched back to the German trench and placed in a large dugout.

> 'No wonder the bastards survived the shelling. Can you believe this place? The fucking walls must be three feet wide. That's a bloody lot of concrete' said Albert.

> 'Yeah and what about the depth? We must have been marched down 40 steps. There's no fucking way one of our shells could have broken through,' responded Roy Williams.

> 'What do you think the Krauts are going to do with us?' asked Mal.

> 'Well they've got two choices, shoot us all or march us off to a POW camp,' said Roy.

> 'I'd prefer the second option,' offered Mal.

> 'Yeah, I think we all would.'

The twenty diggers were kept in the bunker for a further day. The Battle of Fromelles was well and truly finished, and lost. On July 21st German soldiers entered the bunker and ordered the diggers up the stairs. Once they reached ground level they saw several hundred or so Australian POWs.

Directed to march three abreast the prisoners headed towards the German occupied town of Lille twenty miles away.

They arrived in the medieval town by early afternoon.

Australian POWs Marching Through Lille

Australian, British, and French prisoners were all distributed across Germany to various POW camps, some more lenient than others.

Malcolm was dispatched to Warzburg in Northern Bavaria a camp with a reputation for tolerance.

As an ordinary private Malcolm was sent to what the Germans called the *Mannschaftslager* roughly meaning team camp. These were the basic camps made up of wooden barracks.

Warzburg POW Camp 1917

Warzburg POW Camp - Barrack Hut

Each of these barracks kept around 250 prisoners. Furniture was kept to a minimum: a table, chairs or benches and a stove. Camps also featured barracks for guards, a cafeteria or *Kantine* where prisoners could sometimes buy cigarettes and additional food. The camps also included a barrack for packages and mail sorting, a guardhouse and kitchens. The prisoners were put to work and paid at a rate, determined by their skill level, the lowest paid were farm workers, from 16 to 35 Pfennigs a day (a Pfennig equated to 100th of a German Mark).

Small industries paid 30 to 50 Pfennigs a day, while those in heavy industry received from 75 Pfennigs to 1 Mark a day. For the highly skilled and professional POWs the rate was between 2 and 3 Marks a day.

Each camp had its own particular structures, notably sanitary facilities or cultural places like a library, a theatre hall or a place of worship.

Australian POWs

When prisoners were put to work they could occasionally spend periods of time away from their parent camp such as those engaged in agriculture sometimes being housed in village assembly halls.

This is where Malcolm saw out the duration of the war. In 1919 he was shipped back to Australia and resumed life working on the *Murray Princess*.

His older brother Alex had joined the 53rd Division, also participating in The Battle of Fromelles, but had died in the battle. Malcolm only discovered his brother's fate upon returning to Australia.

Forty Thousand Horsemen and One Boy From Walpeup

Chapter 18

Walpeup Victoria 1915

Harry Bell came from a long line of farmers from both the Mallee region of Victoria and Somerset England before his grandfather and grandmother immigrated to Australia in 1890.

Harry was the eldest of seven children; his father Albert and mother Elsie both worked the cattle and cereal crop farm and in most years could sustain their large family and make a modest profit.

This was not the case in 1914; after a dry spring and summer rain fell in April giving the Bells and their neighbours the confidence to sow. Across the Australian wheat-belt, farmers committed themselves to another year's cycle not realising that southern Australia had begun one of the driest periods on record. As 1914 progressed, rainfall ceased and did not return; the ground became drier, vegetation withered and confidence evaporated with the moisture.

The thirteen months from April 1914 to May 1915 remain one of the most severe drought periods in the history of southern Australia. The drought was particularly severe in Victoria, southern-most South Australia, central New South Wales, Tasmania and south-western Western Australia. At the end of this period the wheat harvest was only a quarter of what it had been the previous year.

The Bell farm barely survived, Elsie brought in extra money by becoming a teacher's aid at the local school and all the kids helped around the farm after school hours. Even little three-year-old Bella contributed by collecting the eggs each day.

By 1916 things were getting back to normal; the rains came on time, the pasture was green again, the cereal crops were growing at their normal rate.

Young Harry had grown up on a farm and as a consequence had learned to ride a horse before he could walk. He became a fine horseman competing in horse shows and winning blue ribbons. The most treasured prize was winning at the Mildura Agricultural Show. This he had done for the past three years.

Mildura 1917

April had come around again and the Mildura Show would be held on the 16th and 17th. Harry spent many hours preparing the horse he would ride in the show jumping event making sure Sultan's coat shone and his mane was neatly plaited. His father would transport Sultan and Harry in a horse float pulled by the farm truck. The remainder of the family had to stay home and look after the farm.

The trip to Mildura took three and a half hours, an uncomfortable trip for Harry but Sultan seemed to cope fine.

They entered the show grounds and were guided to their assigned parking area next to the horse stalls where they would stay for the duration. The men and the horse would sleep and eat around this area.

Father and son made sure Sultan was comfortable in his stall, ensured he had plenty of feed and went off to the canteen for their evening meal. Once fed and watered they returned to the stall to check on their prize horse and then hunkered down in the horse float, sleeping on a bed of hay and blankets.

The next day was the first round of show jumping; Harry and Sultan achieved a perfect score going into the next round easily.

The second round was in the afternoon; again both rider and horse completed the circuit without losing a point. The final was to be held the next morning.

Harry and his father secured Sultan away and decided to take in the events in the main arena before dinner. They were both sitting quite close to the fence so they had an excellent view of the proceedings. The last event was announced, the Australian Light Horse would complete a mock cavalry charge.

Light Horse Charging

Harry was enthralled watching these Australian soldiers dressed in their distinctive uniforms galloping across the arena. What an adventure that would be, wielding a sword or a lance, charging the enemy in some far away land.

Father and son went and ate their dinner, returning to Sultan's stall about 8pm. Harry told his Father he would like to go for a walk before retiring for the night and wandered down to the arena, sitting on one of the wooden seats contemplating tomorrow's ride. He heard a noise and looked up to see the Captain from the Light Horse Battalion from the charge they'd watched earlier.

'Good evening lad, would you mind if I sit down by your side for a while?'

'No, certainly Sir.'

'I saw you ride today; you're very good.'

'Thank you, I saw you ride today and so are you.'

The captain laughed.

'Would you be interested in joining the Light Horse? We could certainly use a horseman of your skill.'

'I must admit when I saw that charge today I could imagine myself being a part of it.'

'Sorry, I haven't introduced myself. I'm Captain Gilmore of the 4th Light Horse.'

'I'm Harry Bell of Walpeup.'

'Well Harry what do you think? I could organise you to sign up tomorrow.'

'What would I need to do Captain?'

'Well, you would need to fill in some basic forms and take a medical. I don't think you would have any trouble passing that by the look of you.'

'Is that it?'

'Pretty much, you just need to be over eighteen and willing to fight for King and country.'

'Let me think about it overnight and I'll give you my answer in the morning. Now if you'll excuse me I should get going – I've got a big day tomorrow.'

Harry bid farewell to the Captain and headed back to the horse float to try and get some sleep. He had a lot on his mind.

His father was already asleep and snoring by the time Harry slipped in next to him. The young lad lay there trying not to think about the next day's competition *or* the idea of enlisting in the Light Horse. The main issue would be his age, as at only fifteen he was short a few years. Could he get away with lying about his age? He got very little sleep that night.

The day began with heavy showers, not what the riders or the event organisers had hoped for. The show jumping final was re-scheduled for the afternoon and luckily the rain stopped by mid-morning, allowing the arena to dry out.

Harry was the opening rider and whether it was nerves or horse error the pole was knocked off the first jump.

He completed the remainder of the course without error and felt reasonably happy; not a perfect run but a score to beat for the following riders. By the end of the event Harry had won a blue ribbon, the prestigious silver trophy his for another year. When he returned to the holding yard his father ran up and shook his hand.

'Well done son I'm very proud of you. We'll have a celebration tonight by crikey.'

'Thanks Dad, can you take Sultan for me? I need to talk to a fellow on the other side of the arena.'

Harry went looking for the Light Horse Captain he'd spoken with the night before and found him talking to some new recruits. Harry waited until they finished and then approached the officer.

'Excuse me Captain Gilmore, may I speak with you for a second?'

'Harry, of course you can. That was a splendid effort out there, well done.'

'Thank you Sir, I've decided to try out for the Light Horse if that's OK?'

'Of course it is, when would you like to sign up?'

'Now, if that's possible.'

'Well, the enlistment centre has just closed but for a magnificent rider like you I'm sure we can make an exception.'

'That would be terrific as I'm going home first thing tomorrow.'

Captain Gilmore himself put Harry through the enlistment process, the medical passed with flying colours.

'Right now Harry that's about it, we just have to complete this form. How old did you say you were?'

'Eighteen Sir.'

'Excellent, well Trooper Bell you are now a member of the Australian 4th Light Horse Regiment.'

'Sir, when will I need to report to base?'

'The next recruitment intake is in three weeks.'

Harry returned to the horse float and washed up before dinner. His father let Harry drive the truck into town and shouted them a slap-up meal at the pub. Harry was even allowed beer with his steak.

They rose at 5am and hitched up the horse float, heading for home with the silverware taking pride of place in the passenger's seat of the truck. The two winners travelled in the horse float.

The next few weeks went very slowly for Harry, torn between feelings for his family, commitment to the farm and the knowledge he would be leaving shortly to begin his army training. Harry decided not to mention enlisting to his parents or siblings; he felt it best just to leave and write to them later, explaining his actions after being shipped overseas.

May 27th 1917

Harry woke at 4am, his bag already packed and Sultan saddled and ready to go. Creeping out the back door, carrying his boots to ensure he made as little noise as possible, Harry began his great adventure.

He entered the barn, tied his bag onto the saddle and led his old mate out into the darkness. Harry mounted Sultan and they headed down the farm's long driveway. Harry estimated it would take three days to reach Victoria Barracks in St Kilda Road Melbourne, so they would arrive on the 30th, a day before he was expected to report for duty.

The two travellers reached the small town of Wychproof on the first night where Harry found a nice spot by the river and pitched his tent, tying Sultan to a nearby tree with a bucket of oats and water to keep him going. After cooking up some porridge and making a billy of tea they got underway again, heading for Bendigo and then onto Melbourne.

On schedule after three full days of riding Harry and Sultan arrived at Victoria Barracks. Unsure what to do or where to go, Harry rode Sultan into a large cobblestone courtyard and dismounted. Tying his mate to a veranda post Harry started to search for someone in authority. By coincidence he ran into Captain Gilmore.

> 'Harry! Fancy bumping into you lad you're not due here until tomorrow.'

Harry explained how he'd ridden from Walpeup and wanted to make sure he arrived on time.

> 'That's a fair ride son, but then again a horseman of your skill shouldn't have any trouble coping with three days in the saddle.'

> 'Thank you Sir.'

> 'So Harry, where's your horse now?'

> 'Tied to a post in the big courtyard Sir.'

> 'Is he now? Well we'd better take him to the stables.'

They went and retrieved Sultan and led him to a large stable area where all the horses were kept.

> 'So Harry what do you intend to do with Sultan?'

> 'Well Sir, I was rather hoping I could take him with me.'

'What, as a cavalry horse?'

'Yes Sir, you wouldn't get a finer horse. Not many horses can beat him and as you saw, he can jump.'

'That's a point, although it's highly unusual for a trooper to supply his own horse.'

'Sir, I would really appreciate it if you would consider the idea.'

'Harry, you understand it's more than likely Sultan won't be coming home after the war is over, don't you?'

'Yes Sir, but the same applies to me I suppose.'

'Well I'm sure you'll survive Harry. All right, I'll speak to Major Henderson and see if he'll approve your request. No promises.'

Captain Gilmore showed Harry the barracks he would sleep in and asked one of the regular troopers to give him the full tour and keep an eye out.

In the morning Harry was issued with the Light Horse uniform including the slouch hat with emu plume, leather leggings, and a pair of spurs. Harry felt very proud.

Captain Gilmore summoned Harry to his office in the afternoon informing him that if Sultan passed all the trials each horse had to pass over the course of the six-week training program, he could take Sultan with him. Harry was elated and raced to the stables to inform Sultan of the good news.

Training began on June 1st 1917 and encompassed riding skills, marksmanship, using a bayonet while charging, and many long rides in full kit.

Finally Harry, and his brothers in arms were ready to be shipped out. He had made some very good mates while training but none closer than Jim Bishop, another country boy from Mildura.

On August 1st 1917 Harry and Jim embarked on the HMAT *Hymettus* at Melbourne dock bound for Egypt.

After six weeks at sea and many bouts of seasickness in rough weather the Australian Light Horse 4th Division arrived in Egypt. The troops were transferred to Mena Camp about ten miles out of Cairo.

Mena Camp Cairo 1915

Australian Mascot

The Australians had only seen drawings of the pyramids in books at school. Most of them hadn't been more than fifty miles from their homes so seeing one of the seven wonders of the ancient world was an amazing experience.

What was also amazing was the soldiers' first excursion into Cairo where they saw sights unimaginable at home; painted ladies, camels, goats, and exotic markets selling genuine trinkets from the tombs of the pharaohs.

Sultan coped with the sea voyage very well but was finding the Egyptian heat a little overbearing. Part of Harry and Jim's education was learning new songs composed by the diggers who had been there for some time.

Their favourite was:

> *Land of heat and sweaty socks,*
>
> *Sin and sand and tons of pox,*
>
> *Streets of sorrow, streets of shame,*
>
> *Streets to which we give no name;*
>
> *Harlots, thieves and pestering wogs,*
>
> *Stinks and dirt and sneaking dogs,*
>
> *Flies that drive a man insane,*
>
> *Make him curse with oath profane:*
>
> *Blazing heat and aching feet,*
>
> *Gyppo guts and camel meat,*

Clouds of choking dust that blind,

Drive a man clean off his mind;

The Arab's heaven -- soldier's hell,

Land of Bastards, fare thee well!

Jim was assigned a beautiful chestnut horse called Big Ben he was seventeen hands, taller than a normal light horse but also quicker than most. The boys partook in daily exercises riding with the other troopers of the Battalion. Galloping past the sphinx and pyramids gave the lads a sense of being Arabian knights.

Captain Gilmore called his men together and announced they were departing the next morning to join General Harry Chauvel's Division attack on a critical Turkish stronghold. The Light Horse were heading to Beersheba.

General Chauvel

Beersheba

Chapter 19

The two boys from country Victoria looked at each other and smiled, this is why they joined up; at last they would be tested not only in horsemanship but bravery. Harry and Jim were both ready to prove themselves in battle.

Beersheba

Twenty British Corps comprising of four Divisions amounting to over 60,000 men launched an attack on Beersheba at dawn on October 31st 1917. By late afternoon the corps had made little headway toward the town and its vital water wells. General Harry Chauvel, commanding the Desert Mounted Corps, ordered the 4th Light Horse Brigade forward to attempt to secure the position.

The light horsemen did not carry swords or lances, instead holding their bayonets as swords.

Harry felt nervous as they approached the village, not knowing what level of defence the Turks had; neither did British Intelligence.

Harry, Jim, and about 40,000 Light Horsemen waited on a ridge for the command; at last General Chauvel gave the order to charge.

The Turks must have been terrified; only 1,000 of them defending their position as 40,000 soldiers on horseback charged towards them, bayonets waving and shouting.

When Harry reached the Turkish line, Sultan jumped over the trench but a Turk shot Harry's beloved horse in the chest. Sultan dropped. Harry was pinned beneath his horse and couldn't move. A Turkish officer shot Harry at point blank range in the head; he died instantly.

He was just a boy.

Thirty-eight Turkish and German officers and about 700 other ranks were taken prisoner, and a critical supply of water was secured.

The Australians suffered 67 casualties; 2 officers and 29 men from other ranks were killed, 8 officers and 28 men from other ranks were wounded.

The fall of Beersheba opened the way to outflank the Gaza-Beersheba Line. On November 6th after severe fighting Turkish forces began to withdraw from Gaza pulling back further into Palestine.

Jungle Boy

Chapter 20

Melbourne 1941

Danny Grimshaw was a typical fifteen-year-old boy from Seymour in central Victoria; he loved playing Australian Rules football in the winter and cricket in the summer. Like many boys of his age, he left school in eighth grade to help his family run their dairy farm. Danny came from a small family, his only sibling was a younger sister, Kate, two years his junior.

His father, Tom, came from a long line of dairy farmers and his family had lived in the district since 1872, the same year the railway line opened in Seymour. Tom had fought in the First World War, serving in France and Belgium, but was one of the lucky ones who returned to Australia unscathed, apart from a bout of trench foot.

Nobody really knew what inspired Danny to lie about his age and enlist but his parents suspected he wanted to emulate his father's heroic deeds.

Dear Mum and Dad,

I'm sorry to tell you like this but I felt it was for the best.

I have enlisted in the army and will be trained at an army base for the next twelve weeks before being deployed somewhere overseas.

Dad you enlisted for the first one so you will have some idea why I did what I did.

I've changed my name so even if you wanted to track me down you couldn't.

I promise I will write when I've arrived wherever I'm going so you will know I'm safe.

Say goodbye to Kate for me.

I love you all

Your Son

Danny

His parents were devastated their only son had run away to join the fray, his mother particularly upset as she couldn't imagine what her baby would face fighting a war.

The young boy was assigned to 2/21st Battalion, part of the 23rd Brigade 8th Division. Danny completed his training at Trawool and then transferred to Bonegilla, 150 miles marching with full kit. There was no doubt he was in the army now! Jimmy, the name he was now known by was looking forward to being deployed overseas to some faraway land, just like his father had been in the previous war.

Training had finished on the 23rd March 1941. While the 8th Division's two other brigades, the 22nd and 27th were deployed to Malaya in 1941 to bolster the garrison there. The Australian government decided to keep the 23rd in Australia to deploy to the islands immediately north of Australia – Ambon, Timor, and Rabaul – if war broke out with the Japanese. This plan had the 2/21st Battalion earmarked to reinforce Dutch troops on Ambon if the Japanese decided to attack. As the likelihood of war with Japan increased, the battalion moved to Darwin in the Northern Territory, the closest port for sending troops to Ambon.

Darwin, Australia. April 1941

The 2/21st Battalion was shipped to Darwin arriving in April 1941. It was here that young Jimmy and his newfound mates spent the next nine months.

Newly Arrived 2/21st Battalion

'So this is why we joined the fucking army? We're fighting fucking flies and mossies not the bloody Japanese,' complained Rick Hansen.

'Yeah this place is the pits. Hardly what you'd call an army camp,' agreed Rob Hill.

'I still can't believe we had to build the fucking place ourselves. I don't think there's too many camps where you have to do that.'

Not only did the Battalion have to construct their own huts, their location 17.5 miles from the Darwin town centre was a prohibitive distance for the boys to visit the town. The camp was aptly named 17.5 Mile Camp.

After numerous marches in the tropical heat with full pack and many hours of boredom the Battalion received orders to ship out to Ambon on December 17th as part of Gull Force commanded by Lieutenant Colonel Leonard Roach.

Gull Force consisted of the 2/21st Battalion supported by anti-tank artillery, engineers, and other support; a combined strength of 1,100 men. Meanwhile, Netherlands East Indies forces on the island numbered some 2,600 men, including several companies of Indonesian troops and Dutch coastal artillery. These troops were tasked with defending the Bay of Ambon and the airfields at Laha and Liang, which were being used by a few Dutch and some Australian aircraft from No. 13 Squadron RAAF.

With the small Australian and Dutch forces totalling just 3,700 men, Colonel Roach believed the limited military resources would be unable to defend Ambon and urgently requested reinforcements. As a consequence he was relieved of his command and replaced by Lieutenant Colonel William Scott on January 17th 1942. Scott altered the location of many defensive positions, which resulted in the battalion's defences being weakened just prior to the Japanese landing on the island.

January 31st 1942

'You know what mate, I'm a bit bloody nervous. What about you?' said Jimmy.

'I'm not nervous mate, I'm bloody shit scared,' replied Rob.

'I wonder why Roach pissed off?'

'I have a feeling he had no say in the matter. It was more likely General Blamey's doing.'

'Anyway, we should be concentrating on spotting Japs not speculating about what goes on in high command.'

'OK lads, we've just received word from our spotters that the Japs have landed on both the north and south coasts and are making their way here. Make sure your rifles are clean, you have a full magazine and fix your bayonets,' instructed Captain Spargo. We want to be ready to give them an appropriate greeting.'

The Japanese were intent on capturing Ambon, landing with their 38th Division, a Marine Battalion, and the Special Naval Landing Force.

On the very first day of fighting the Dutch forces surrendered to the Japanese leaving the Australian forces outnumbered, without air or naval support. Unable to defend Ambon, the Australians were forced to retreat to the far west of the peninsula.

Companies B and C, Jimmy's group, were charged with defending Laha Airfield.

The Japanese attacked the airfield in strength. Despite fighting gallantly the 2/21st battalion could not hold back the Japanese, finally surrendering to their force, superior not only in numbers but also experience.

Approximately 150 Australians were captured and interned, held in a barbed wire enclosure with no shelter from the intense tropical sun.

'What do you think they'll do with us mate?' Jimmy asked.

'Buggered if I know cobber. I suppose they'll transport us to a luxurious POW camp where we can laze about all day and play the odd game of tennis,' jested Rob.

'In your dreams Rob, based on what I've seen so far I think we're in for a rough trot.'

'Yeah, I think you're right mate.'

'Hey mate do you know what day it is today?'

'Dunno. About the 1st of February I reckon. Why?'

'It's my birthday.'

'You're kidding me, happy birthday mate. How old?'

'Well, I guess its OK to tell you now. I'm sixteen.'

'Bullshit, you can't be sixteen. They wouldn't have let you join up.'

'I lied about my age and changed my name.'

'What's your real name then?'

'Danny.'

'Is there anything else you'd like to share with me? You're not a girl are you?'

'No, of course not.'

Just then, four Japanese soldiers approached and ordered them to join about 50 other POWs and follow. They were marched out of the compound and taken to the far end of the airfield. Waiting to greet them were a few dozen Japanese soldiers with bayonets and military swords.

'What the fuck's going on here? These bastards look like they mean to kill us,' said Rob.

'They can't do that, it's against the Geneva Convention,' replied Jimmy.

The diggers were unaware Japan didn't recognise the convention or indeed other principles of human decency in war.

'Mate they couldn't give a fuck about the rules, they do what they bloody well like.'

'There's more of us. Let's try and overpower the bastards and make a run for it,' said Jimmy.

'Take a look at them Jimmy, they're armed to the teeth and we have our hands tied. There's no way out of this.'

'Well we can't just stand here and be killed. We've got to do something. Fucked if I'm going to die on my birthday.'

The senior Japanese officer demanded that all talking cease, instructing his assassins to line up the POWs in two rows of 25 prisoners.

Rob was in that first row and the Japs lined up behind them. When the order was given the diggers received a bayonet in the back with such force the bayonet protruded through their chests and they slumped to the ground. Standing over the fallen diggers the Japanese continued stabbing the wounded soldiers until they were unrecognizable as human beings. Watching in horror, the remaining 25 Australians were instructed to kneel on the ground with straight backs.

Several officers, including the commander, drew their swords and one by one decapitated the defenceless diggers.

Jimmy was shaking and tears were rolling down his face. He prayed and just before the sword struck yelled out 'Mother'.

The 50 soldiers were buried in a mass grave by the Japanese murderers, all volunteers.

Further massacres occurred over the next few days. In total more than 300 died.

Jimmy died on his sixteenth birthday. He was just a boy.

Ambon Massacre

I Want to be Like My Dad

Chapter 21

Joseph Buchanan's father, Roy, fought in the First World War, suffering shrapnel wounds to his right leg that necessitated it being amputated in a field hospital in Ypres. Roy was a policeman before the war but being disabled meant he couldn't return to the force. He became a postal clerk in Richmond, which he detested – although he remained there for the rest of his working life. Now his son Joseph was just about to embark on his own adventure, after enlisting with the army at Victoria Barracks in Melbourne.

Joseph was sixteen. His parents had no idea he had lied about his age, enlisting under an assumed surname. The date was February 20th 1942. Singapore had just fallen to the Japanese and Australia was calling on its finest to hold back the peril from Australian shores. Enlistment officers became a lot less diligent about checking birth certificates because the army was desperate for new recruits.

Young Joseph now answered to the name of Joseph Irvine. He reported for duty at Victoria Barracks and was transported to Puckapunyal Army Base for his eight-week training program.

North of Australia New Guinea was facing an emergency, with the Japanese heading for Port Moresby at breakneck speed.

The training schedule was reduced. After only four weeks Joseph hadn't even mastered the use of his rifle, let alone how to care for it among the jungle conditions he was about to endure. Transferred to Melbourne Joseph and fellow troops were hastily loaded onto a troop ship, the *Aquitania*, sailing to Port Moresby to face the battle-hardened Japanese, by now a very experienced army.

Joseph had never been on a ship and before long seasickness became a major problem in the open seas.

Finally the *Aquitania* berthed at Port Moresby. Once the ship was secured and gangplanks lowered the soldiers disembarked in an orderly fashion.

What wasn't orderly or well planned was the loading of the ship's hold prior to leaving Melbourne. The tents and food supplies had been loaded first and were therefore the last items to be unloaded.

On their first night in Port Moresby the 39th Battalion were forced to sleep out in the open and had no rations to eat. Back in Melbourne a logistics officer had a lot to answer for.

Things were about to get worse though as the 39th Battalion were heading for the Kokoda Track.

'ANZAC created a nation; Kokoda saved a nation.'
His Excellency David Irvine, Australian High Commissioner to Papua New Guinea, 1998

The Fuzzy Wuzzy Angels

By the end of June 1942, the Japanese plan to isolate Australia from the United States was well advanced. Japan was establishing a major base at the port of Lae on the mainland coast of Australia's Territory of New Guinea. Japanese naval landing forces had occupied Buka, Bougainville and Shortland, which are the three northernmost islands of the Solomon Islands chain. Between May and July 1942, the Japanese progressively occupied more of the islands comprising the Solomon Islands chain. As each island was occupied, the Japanese built forward airstrips in pursuance of their plan to intercept military aid for Australia from the United States.

135

By the middle of July 1942, Japan had occupied the southern island of Guadalcanal in the Solomons chain, and 2,000 Japanese troops and construction workers were engaged in building the airstrip, which would later be known as Henderson Field.

The next step in the Japanese plan to isolate Australia from the United States would be the capture of Port Moresby on the southern coast of Australia's Territory of Papua. Port Moresby was of vital importance to Japan. With the whole of the island of New Guinea and the Solomon Islands under Japanese control, Japan could establish naval bases and forward airfields on these territories from which it could strike deeply into the Australian mainland and intercept military support for Australia from the United States.

The Japanese had initially intended to capture Port Moresby in April 1942, but American carrier-launched aircraft from USS Lexington and USS Yorktown on 10 March 1942 and smashed the invasion fleet that the Japanese were assembling at Lae. The Japanese were forced to postpone the capture of Port Moresby until May 1942. When the Japanese finally launched a powerful seaborne invasion force towards Port Moresby in the first week of May 1942, their first attempt to capture Port Moresby was frustrated by a joint United States and Australian naval task force at the Battle of the Coral Sea. For the first time in the Pacific War, a Japanese invasion fleet was forced to withdraw, and Australia was saved from more intensive aerial bombardment and a grave threat to aid from the United States.

Despite these setbacks, the Japanese were still determined to capture Port Moresby. The Imperial Japanese Navy had operational responsibility for Japanese military operations in the South-West Pacific area, but with the loss of four of its six best aircraft carriers at Midway, and Shokaku badly damaged at the Battle of the Coral Sea, the Japanese Navy was no longer capable of mounting a seaborne invasion of Port Moresby. Faced with this dilemma, Japan's admirals decided to pass the task of capturing Port Moresby to the Japanese Army.

Japan's military strategists developed a plan for the capture of Port Moresby which involved a two prong attack. Tough jungle-trained troops of the Japanese South Seas Detachment, under the command of Major General Tomitaro Horii, would land near the villages of Gona and Buna on the northern coast of Papua, seize the airstrip at Kokoda, and cross the Owen Stanley Range by means of the Kokoda Track. Once over the mountains of the Owen Stanley Range, Port Moresby would lie open to attack and capture by the Japanese troops. The second prong of the attack would involve a landing by Japanese marines at Milne Bay on the eastern tip of Papua where Australians and Americans had been building a forward airbase since 28 June 1942. When captured, Milne Bay would provide Japan with an air and naval base from which Major General Horii's attack on Port Moresby could be supported by Japanese aircraft and seaborne invasion troops.

The task of crossing the Owen Stanley Range must have appeared deceptively simple to Japanese military planners studying maps in Tokyo. They had never seen this massive, rugged central mountain feature of the island of New Guinea, which separates the northern coast of Papua from the southern coast.

The dense tropical jungles and heavy rainfall of New Guinea provided harsh conditions for soldiers who fought there in the Pacific War. The first Australians to arrive in New Guinea faced elite Japanese troops of the South Seas Detachment on the Kokoda Track and crack Japanese marines of the Special Naval Landing Forces at Milne Bay. These tough Japanese troops had acquired extensive combat experience fighting in China, Malaya, the Philippines, and Dutch East Indies. They were experienced jungle fighters, and the dense jungles of New Guinea provided them with ideal conditions for their kind of fighting.

The Australians on the Kokoda Track were heavily outnumbered, ill-equipped, poorly supplied, inadequately trained for jungle warfare, and fighting a fiercely determined enemy. To add to their problems, conditions on the Kokoda Track were appalling. The narrow dirt track climbed steep heavily timbered mountains, and then descended into deep valleys choked with dense rain forest. The steep gradients and the thick vegetation made movement difficult, exhausting, and at times dangerous. Razor-sharp kunai grass tore at their clothing and slashed their skin.

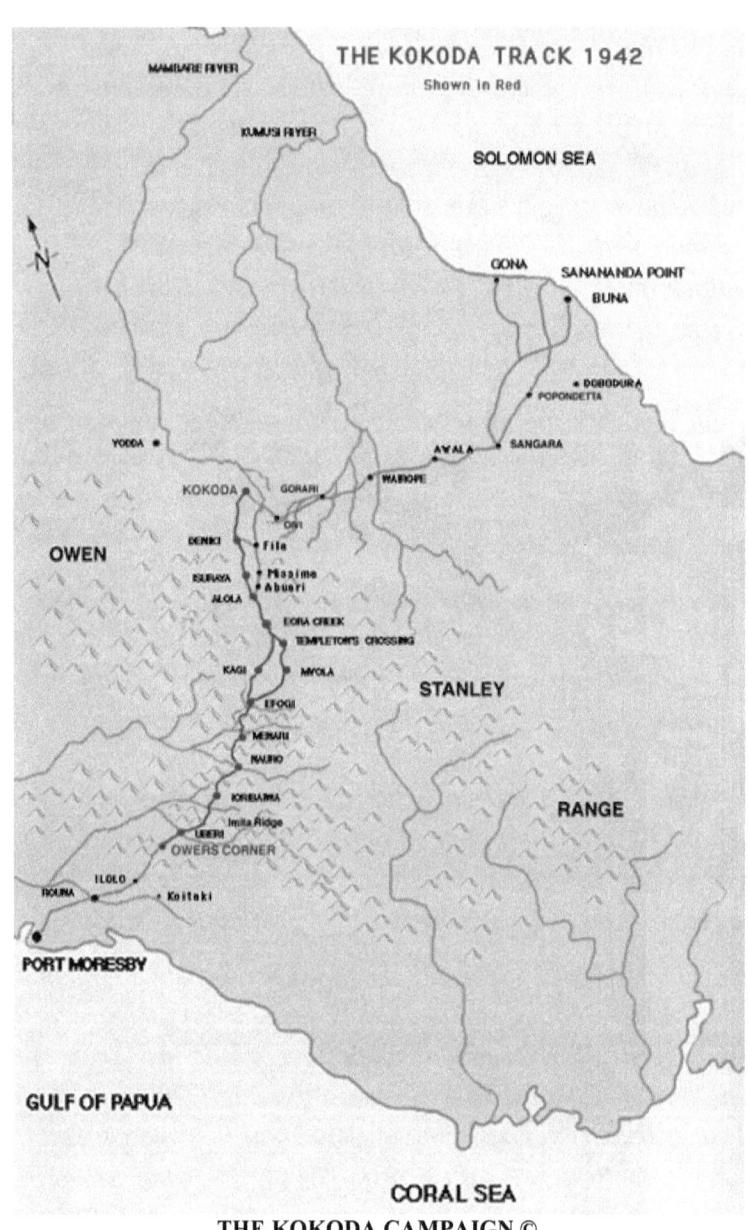

THE KOKODA CAMPAIGN ©

In many parts of the island of New Guinea, including the areas where the Kokoda Campaign was fought, the average annual rainfall is about 5 metres (16 feet), and daily rainfalls of 25 centimetres (10 inches) are not uncommon. When these rains fell, dirt tracks quickly dissolved into calf-deep mud, which exhausted the soldiers after they had struggled several hundred metres through it and bogged military vehicles to the axles.

138

Sluggish streams in mountain ravines quickly became almost impassable torrents when the rains began to fall.

Re-supply was a nightmare for the Australian commanders on the Kokoda Track, because every item of food, ammunition and equipment had to be manhandled along the track or dropped by air. Heat, oppressive humidity, mosquitoes, and leeches added to the discomfort of the rain-drenched Australian soldiers who were often without adequate food and even a cup of tea. As if this was not enough for the Australian diggers to face, their other deadly enemy was disease. Malaria, dengue fever, scrub typhus, and dysentery flourished in these conditions and added to the misery of the exhausted Australians. Wet clothes and boots were a frequent source of unpleasant skin diseases.

Australian Militia Battalions are sent to guard Australia's northern approaches

In response to ominous signs in 1941 that Japan was preparing for military aggression in the South-West Pacific region, the Australian government undertook a rapid expansion of Australia's volunteer Citizen Military Forces, also known as the militia, for the defence of the Australian mainland and overseas territories. Although liable to be called up to defend Australia, these militia troops were inadequately trained, and lacked adequate equipment and weapons.

Between March and December 1941, the Australian Government moved three militia battalions to Port Moresby to defend this vital northern gateway to Australia. The average age of these militia recruits was eighteen and a half years. Unlike the second Australian Imperial Force (2nd AIF), which had been recruited to fight the Germans and Italians in Europe and North Africa, the military service of the militia soldiers was strictly limited to the defence of Australia and its island Territories.

To many in the 2nd AIF, who could not foresee Japan's entry into World War II on the side of Germany and Italy in December 1941, the militia wore the uniforms of soldiers but without the risk of ever being involved in combat. This distinction between AIF and militia service led to the young militia recruits being branded "chocolate soldiers" or "chocos" by some AIF members. The scornful term "choco" was intended to convey a suggestion that the militia recruits would melt if exposed to the pressures of real combat. As if to underline their second-class status in the eyes of many senior AIF commanders, the militia recruits were denied adequate *training and equipment, and treated with a cavalier disregard for their welfare and feelings. These attitudes produced ill feeling between the AIF and the militia, which Australia could simply not afford.*

Although initially a volunteer citizen army, following the fall of Singapore on 15 February 1942, the Curtin Labor government ordered full mobilisation on 19 February 1942. Thereafter, all males aged 18-35, and all single males aged 35-45, became liable to conscription into the militia. During the first half of 1942, the Commander of the 8th Military District, Major General Morris, had no experienced AIF troops under his command at Port Moresby. His main force was the 30th Australian Infantry Brigade, a militia formation comprising the 39th, 49th and 53rd Australian Infantry Battalions. With the exception of the 53rd Battalion, the militia were led by experienced AIF officers and NCOs but the troops were almost all raw recruits.

The appalling treatment of these young militia recruits provides a damning indictment of Australia's Army leadership in 1941-42. None of these militia units had received proper military training before arriving at Port Moresby. The 49th Battalion reached Port Moresby in March 1941 without the most basic infantry equipment, and were immediately put to work as labourers - unloading ships, and constructing roads and buildings. The 39th and 53rd Battalions reached Port Moresby on the Aquitania in January 1942, and they could not immediately be fed and sheltered because their food supplies and camping equipment had been stowed at the bottom of the ship's hold. Many of the raw recruits of the 53rd Battalion had never handled a rifle until they were put on board the ship bound for Port Moresby. The 39th Battalion, which had been raised in Victoria in October 1941, was fortunate in that it had more experienced AIF officers than the other two militia battalions.

The important role played by Australian Militia troops in New Guinea

Despite their lack of adequate training, equipment and supplies, and despite the appalling conditions under which they fought in New Guinea, the heavily outnumbered militia soldiers of the 39th Australian Infantry Battalion would play a critical and heroic role in delaying the momentum of the Japanese advance along the Kokoda Track towards Port Moresby until seasoned AIF reinforcements could be brought into the battle.

Local units available to support the Australian Militia at Port Moresby

In addition to the Australian militia units, General Morris also had troops of the local Papuan Infantry Battalion (PIB) and the local New Guinea Volunteer Rifles (NGVR). The troops of the NGVR, all European and numbering about 450, were spread thinly across areas of the Australian Territory of New Guinea not occupied by the Japanese. The fortifications of Port Moresby in April 1942 comprised two ancient naval guns, a field artillery regiment, a heavy anti-aircraft battery, and a few mobile anti-aircraft guns.

Composition of an infantry battalion on the Kokoda Track in 1942

It is appropriate to mention at this point the composition of an infantry battalion because references will be made from time to time to the components of a battalion when dealing with land battles on the island of New Guinea.

In 1942, an Australian Imperial Force (AIF) infantry battalion was composed of several companies, usually four rifle companies and a headquarters company, and designated respectively: A, B, C, D and HQ. Militia battalions often included a fifth machine-gun company designated E. Each rifle company was composed of three platoons, which were identified by numbers starting from one. On the Kokoda Track, the number of troops in each of the components of an infantry battalion could vary significantly, and it is convenient to think in terms of a range of 450-550 soldiers when battalions are mentioned, about 100-110 for a rifle company, and about 30-35 for a rifle platoon.

The Australian Government recalls AIF Divisions to defend Australia

The surrender to the Japanese of Britain's so-called "impregnable fortress" of Singapore, and the seemingly inexorable advance of Japanese military forces across the South-West Pacific, caused the Australian Government in February 1942 to recall Australia's AIF 6th and 7th Divisions from the Middle East. When Singapore fell, Britain's Prime Minister Winston Churchill made it very clear to Australian Prime Minister John Curtin that Britain's highest priority was the defence of India, "The Jewel in the (British) Crown", and that no British soldiers would be provided for the defence of Australia against a Japanese invasion. As if to underline his apparent lack of concern for the fate of Australia, Churchill tried to divert the AIF troops to Burma when they were returning by sea to Australia. If the Australian AIF troops had been diverted to Burma they would almost certainly have been lost in another British Far East debacle, and Australia would have been under much greater threat from Japan. Although subjected to verbal bullying by Churchill, Prime Minister Curtin was resolute, and insisted that the Australian AIF troops be allowed to return and defend their own country from a threatened Japanese invasion.

On their return to Australia in March 1942, these seasoned AIF veterans were not sent to New Guinea to defend Port Moresby against a very real threat of Japanese attack, but were kept in Australia to defend the mainland against a possible Japanese invasion. The 7th Division was initially deployed on the coast just north of Brisbane to defend the so-called 'Brisbane Line'.

http://www.pacificwar.org.au/

The 39th Set Off Along the Kokoda Track

The Boys Cooling Down

Jungle Warfare

Chapter 22

Joe and his battalion were not impressed with the torrential rain that first morning, the humidity was hovering around 90 per cent. The 39th helped unload the ship, they didn't complain as at least they were closer to the food supplies and would get to eat. Once everything was unloaded Captain Sam Templeton the battalion commander ordered the cooks to prepare a hearty breakfast for his men. Eggs and bacon with toast and tea was going to be the best tucker they would eat for a good while.

Captain Templeton checked the supplies of weapons and food rations before deciding how much weight each of his charges would carry on the track. Because the Kokoda Track was so remote, supplies would be difficult to get through to the troops and each digger was required to carry extremely heavy packs and equipment. The minimum weight carried by each man was about 40lb (or 18kg) but with a 303 Lee Enfield rifle and other battalion equipment rotated among the men, the burden for each soldier could reach as much as 60lb, approximately 27kg. Burdened with heavy packs, rifles, and ammunition, they were also wearing khaki uniforms more suited to desert warfare than a jungle killing-ground like the Kokoda Track.

Templeton and his troops set out on July 7th 1942 to cross the highland mountains between them and the Kokoda.

Joseph wasn't used to carrying such weight on his back but knew everybody else was struggling with the same burden. At the time, he and his brothers in arms could not have realised that they were marching into history, establishing the foundation of Australia's Kokoda legend.

Joe had teamed up with two other young blokes, Marty and Steve, all sitting down on their packs having a smoke at the front of the Port Moresby Post Office, their starting point for the march into the Owen Stanley mountain range.

The order was given by Captain Templeton to head toward the far end of the town in the direction of the infamous Kokoda Track.

'God knows what it's going to be like climbing mountains with all the shit we have to carry. It's hard enough on level ground,' complained Steve.

'You'll be right mate, I'm sure we'll get used to it,' reassured Joe.

'I hope you're bloody right,' said Marty.

The young, inexperienced 39th were filled with trepidation as they marched for hours along the dirt roads of Port Moresby and beyond.

They reached the beginning of the track at 5pm the following day. Captain Templeton decided they should camp for the night and tackle the track in the morning.

Around the campfire there was plenty of discussion on what might lay ahead. One thing they all agreed upon was their enthusiasm to shoot some Japs, maybe even bayonet a few. Brave talk that would soon be tested.

Reveille was at 5am, their breakfast of corned beef and biscuits at 6am and at 7am their torturous trek began.

As soon as the track started the jungle engulfed them, muddy from continual rain and the slope so steep many soldiers lost their footing and had to be rescued by their mates.

After trudging along the track for ten tortuous days the 39th arrived at the Kokoda airfield exhausted. Their work was about to begin.

Taking a Well Earned Rest

Joseph wrote a letter to his parents in Melbourne describing the conditions. It was the first communication with them since he'd enlisted. The young soldier felt it was time to let them know where he was, having survived the trek to Kokoda.

Joseph on the Kokoda Track

February 3 1942

Dear Mum and Dad,

I've just arrived at a place called Kokoda in Papua New Guinea. We've been marching in the most terrible conditions for the past ten days just to get to this little tinpot place.

Two days after we berthed at Port Moresby we started out on what they call the Kokoda Track. As soon as you hit the track the jungle engulfs you. The first section was downhill all the way and I mean downhill - a decline of 2,500 feet!! The place never stops raining and the track is just mud so you slip and slide all the way down. A couple of blokes hurt themselves pretty bad and had to be carried on stretchers by the fuzzie wuzzies, that's what the local natives are called by all of us. Good blokes and great workers.

It took us the best part of a day to get down this monster mountain track and we camped at the bottom of a ridge called 'Imita'. I've got no idea what that means. We made shelters out of bits of the jungle - palm fronds and tree branches etc. Didn't help much, the insects were unrelenting the little bastards. I got bitten all over as did everybody else. Next morning, after a delicious breakfast of corned beef, biscuits and tea we had to climb up the other side of the mountain, all 2,800 feet of it. Carrying packs up a ridge like that is no easy task, I can tell you. Everyone needed to rest for five minutes each time we climbed a few hundred feet.

Your legs ache, your backaches, and you're soaking wet. The ridge was only about 50 feet wide so had to go down a bit to a plateau where we camped for the night. By the time I reached the campsite my legs were all wobbly. Apparently they call it 'laughing knees' but as far as I'm concerned it was no laughing matter. I could hardly walk.

We'd just got settled in that night when a bloody big storm hit us. I've never seen rain or lightning like it and the thunder - must have sounded like the big guns you had to endure in your time Dad.

Our tents got completely soaked so we slept in puddles for the rest of the night.

We haven't sighted any Japs yet. Mind you that's not to say they're not out there watching every move we make while waiting for the right opportunity.

What's frustrating is that after walking 8 or 10 miles, all bloody day, we arrive at the next camp totally exhausted and then realise that as the crow flies, on the map we're only two miles closer. The whole day's walk is up and down, up and down.

Our next camp was a native grass hut. It had no walls though so the rain just poured in and everybody got soaked, again. It was bitterly cold too because our elevation was about four thousand feet. So there I was wet and cold in a jungle hut with little shelter from the rain. What else could go wrong?

Native rats biting my hair and scratching my nose _plus_ insects eating me alive - that's what.

That first week was just more of the same - climbing and descending, climbing and descending. The pack seems to be getting heavier and heavier and my uniform hasn't been dry since I left Moresby.

But at last we made it to Kokoda safe and sound however the fighting will start any minute. Don't worry - I'll keep my head down..

Your son

Joseph

23 July 1942

Captain Templeton assessed the chances of his men holding back a Japanese attack on the lightly defended airfield. He wasn't confident. Army intelligence had informed him that 2,000 Japanese troops had landed at Gona and were heading their way. The decision was made to send the 11th Platoon back to the Wairopi River with orders to retreat further to Gorari if they encountered any sign of Japanese troops.

> 'Hey Joe, what's with *fall back if you see any Japs?* I thought we were here to beat the shit out of the bastards, not scamper back to safety with our tails between our legs when we see one of the little yellow pricks,' said Ken.

> 'Yeah, I know what you're talking about mate. It seems bloody stupid to me,' answered Joe.

'Shut up you two. I think I just saw some Japs over the other side of the river,' whispered Steve.

'Steve, crawl over to Templeton and let him know,' whispered Joe in reply.

Steve kept low trying not to make any noise as he crawled through the jungle foliage.

Captain Templeton was using high-powered field glasses scouring the river and the bush beyond.

'Sir we've spotted some Japs coming up river, any instructions?'

'Continue to stay low and don't fire unless fired upon. We have no idea how many there are. My guess is they're the forward party for the group that landed at Gona. If that's the case they'll have plenty of back up if we engage them now.'

At that moment the two Australians heard gunfire.

'My God they've spotted us, return their fire then we need to get the hell out of here.'

Steve Firing on the Japanese

The platoon along with Major Watson's Papa troops withdrew to Gorari to join the 12th Platoon. The Australians suffered no casualties and five Japanese were shot dead.

24 July 1942

Captain Templeton, Lieutenant Colonel Owen and their troops arrived in Gorai early on the morning of July 24th to join forces with the 11th and 12th Platoons.

The two officers were expecting reinforcements at Kokoda so decided to try and slow the Japanese advance by setting up an ambush on the track leading from the Kumusi River to Gorari.

They then returned to Kokoda to welcome the reinforcements coming in from Port Moresby.

The ambush didn't delay the Japanese advance for long and 500 of the Japanese 144th Regiment, all jungle warfare veterans, continued in pursuit of the two Australian platoons.

The Australians fought a valiant rear guard withdrawal down the track to the village of Oivi where they intended to make a stand against the approaching enemy.

Although Lieutenant Colonel Owen knew C-Company from his battalion were on their way to Kokoda these troops were still six days away and with the Japanese advancing so rapidly he feared for the airstrip. When he made radio contact with Port Moresby that night, Owen informed Major General Morris of the dire situation and requested two of his rifle companies be flown in to Kokoda the following morning, a twenty-minute flight.

July 26th 1942

An aircraft landed at Kokoda and over two separate flights dropped a platoon of D Company from the 39th Battalion. Despite these efforts the small plane had only delivered fifteen men, all immediately deployed to reinforce the two platoons at Oivi.

Morris did not dispatch any additional reinforcements to Kokoda.

That morning the Japanese aggressively attacked the beleaguered Australians giving the boys a taste of Japanese jungle fighting – a taste that stayed with them for the remainder of the campaign.

The Japanese came in waves. With seemingly no regard for their own lives they were expendable; Emperor Hirohito of Japan owned the life of every soldier.

> 'Fucking hell mate, I reckon I've killed twenty of the little bastards and they just keep coming,' screamed Steve.

> 'Yeah me too, how many of the pricks are out there? Must be hundreds,' replied Joe. 'Shit my gun's jammed.'

> 'Grab that bloke's. It looks like he won't need it any more,' responded Steve.

Joe got up to retrieve the dead man's 303 and a bullet hit him in the centre of his forehead. He wasn't breathing when he hit the ground.

The sixteen-year-old soldier from Richmond Victoria would be buried in a foreign land.

Joe's letter from Kokoda arrived at his parent's home a month after they'd received notification of their son's death.

Hitler's Boys and Girls

Chapter 23

Berlin, Germany. 1942

The Fielders were a middle-class Berlin family living in a middle-class suburb of Schoenberg. Dirk and Jana Fielder were happily married with two young children, Wilhelm aged thirteen and his sister Eva, aged twelve.

Dirk Fielder was an engineer working on a top-secret weapon code named *Vergeltungswaffen.* All senior personnel were required to be fully paid-up members of the Nazi Party. When production began for the weapon it was called the V2 Rocket.

Although Dirk wanted Germany to win the war he was increasingly concerned about Hitler's actions against the Jewish population, including some of Dirk's friends and colleagues before the war.

As a member of the Nazi party he had access to Hitler's plans to control and remove the Jews.

1942

20 January – Wannsee conference in Berlin where Nazis decide that the "final solution" to the Jewish problem is relocation, and subsequently extermination.

17 March – The Nazi German extermination camp Bełżec opened in occupied Poland between March 1942 and December 1942; at least 434,508 people were murdered.

24 March – The deportation of Slovak Jews to Auschwitz began.

27 March – The first French Jews were deported to Auschwitz.

April – The Nazi German extermination camp Sobibor opened in occupied Poland. Between April 1942 and October 1943, at least 160,000 people were murdered.

Spring – The Nazi German extermination camp Treblinka opened in occupied Poland. Between July 1942 and October 1943, around 850,000 people were killed

Dirk couldn't discuss his concerns with anyone except his wife Jana for fear of being turned in to the Gestapo.

The German army had been victorious in almost every battle leading up to the Christmas period of 1942 – by then a large part of Europe was under Nazi domination. Then Hitler attempted to take Stalingrad but after a protracted siege the city didn't fall and German troops went on the defensive. This was the beginning of the end for Hitler and his murderous regime.

Berlin 1943

Wilhelm walked into the lounge room looking as proud as punch after receiving an exceptional honour, The Golden Hitler Youth Badge.

> 'Wilhelm congratulations my son. How did you earn such a medal?'

> 'I heard one of the other boys talking to his friend about the fact that his family were hiding Jews in their basement. I reported what I'd heard to my leader and he informed the Gestapo. As it turned out there were filthy Jews hiding in their house and they were all taken away.'

> 'I see, very well done.'

Dirk did not disclose his true feelings about what his son had done. Young Wilhelm had just signed the death warrant for another two German families.

The Golden Hitler Youth Badge

1944

The highlight of Wilhelm's year was the two-week summer camp in Bavaria, while his younger sister attended a similar camp for girls in Jagerbude, thirty kilometres from Berlin.

Wilhelm joined 2,000 Hitler Youth members hiking, kayaking, and enjoying a range of other physical activities. Hitler was more interested in developing the physical rather than the intellectual strengths of Germany's youth.

The boys slept in huts or tents both accommodating several individuals.

Wilhelm was allocated a bed in one of the huts and was just about asleep when the boy in the next bed spoke.

'Hey Wilhelm, have you heard what's happening tomorrow?'

'No, what Gunther?'

'We're going to the rifle range.'

'Really, are they going to teach us how to fire a rifle?'

'That's what I heard.'

'Who told you?'

'Frederick.'

'He should know.'

'I'm looking forward to that, I'm a bit sick of hiking through the forest.'

'Me too, not to mention the human pyramids and tunnel ball.'

Next morning one hundred of the older boys were marched five kilometres to a firing range normally used by the army.

There were three instructors, all SS, the Nazi special force.

'Boys, today you become men. Once you have mastered the art of shooting you will never be the same again. This will be your first step in defending our beloved Fuhrer and Germany.'

The boys were given instructions from an SS marksman and then twenty by twenty they were handed a Karabiner 98K, the standard rifle used by the army.

'I want you all to pretend you are firing at the enemy. They could be British, French, or even Jews.'

Boys at Rifle Practice

Wilhelm was one of the boys selected as a promising rifleman. Ten boys in all were chosen and told they would receive tuition every day.

Apart from rifle practice the Hitler Youth boys were taught National Socialism and a deep-seated hatred for the Jews.

Jagerbude 1944

Eva also enjoyed summer camp, where the girls of the Young Girls League (BDM), the female equivalent of the Hitler Youth, were marched many kilometres and partook in a variety of sports including swimming and running.

Hitler wanted his girls to take care of their bodies so they could bear as many children as the State needed and to be loyal to National Socialism.

Once Eva completed her time in the BDM she was partway entitled to go to university or into a good job. However, before this could be done she had to compete a year's land service – the so-called *Landfrauenjahr*. This again was an extension of Hitler's belief that true Germans were associated with the land – the belief in blood and soil.

An alternate route, one taken by Eva, was to work with children in a kindergarten. Again, this fulfilled part of Hitler's belief that young women needed to be associated with children. What better way than to look after them when they were very young?

Wilhelm & Eva at 17 and 15

Loyalty to the Fuhrer

Chapter 24

Dirk was sitting in his study sharing a bottle of Schnapps with his dear friend Helmut Bauer, both were engineers working on the V2 Rocket project.

'Tell me Dirk, are you happy the way things are going with the war?'

'To tell you the truth Helmut I think we're looking down the barrel of a massive defeat. Hitler seems to think the V2 will save his bacon but you and I both know it's going to take a lot more than a rocket bomb to win this war.'

'We should have never attacked Russia, I really don't know what he was thinking.'

'True, that was a disaster but it's not just Russia.'

'Yes and as we all know he has total control over every military action. Hitler's not known for taking notice of his Generals, it's his way or no way.'

'I'm afraid if someone doesn't get rid of him Germany is doomed.'

'As much as I hate to say it, I think you're right.'

Unbeknownst to the two men Wilhelm had his ear to the door and heard everything they said.

The next morning Wilhelm didn't attend school and instead made his way to Gestapo head quarters. He asked to speak to a senior officer on the basis he had uncovered an assassination plot against the Fuhrer.

After waiting for ninety minutes finally Wilhelm was ushered into a Gestapo captain's office.

'Sit down young man,' Captain Mahler instructed. 'What's your name?'

'Wilhelm Fielder Sir.'

'Well Wilhelm, I am told you have uncovered a plot to murder our Fuhrer.'

'Yes Sir.'

'Tell me about it.'

'I heard two men say that the Fuhrer should be assassinated because he was an incompetent leader.'

'Did they say how they planned to assassinate the Fuhrer?'

'No Sir, but they made it very clear that Hitler should be eliminated.'

'Wilhelm where did you hear this plot?'

'In my house Sir.'

'Your house?'

'Yes Sir, in my Father's study.'

'Who were these men boy?'

'My father and his friend Helmut Bauer.'

'Wilhelm do you know what will happen to your father if these allegations are proven?'

'Yes Sir, he'll be shot.'

'What's your address and where does your father work?'

Wilhelm gave the Captain all the details.

'You are a very brave and loyal member of the Hitler Youth. I will see to it you receive the highest honour for your actions.'

The young boy left the Gestapo building feeling very proud of his actions – he had demonstrated total dedication to the Fuhrer.

At midnight the Gestapo banged on the front door of the Fielder home. Eventually a sleepy Dirk came down the stairs in his dressing gown and opened the door. Captain Mahler and six Gestapo troops entered, instructing Dirk to show them into the drawing room where he heard the allegations against him.

Protesting his innocence was to no avail. Dirk was handcuffed and led away while from the hallway his wife Jana and two children watched him go.

Captain Mahler looked back and thanked young Wilhelm for his help. Horrified, Jana and Eva looked at Wilhelm as he smiled, saluted and said 'Heil Hitler'.

When Hitler heard of the committed young man who had betrayed his own father to protect the Fuhrer he arranged to meet Wilhelm and awarded him another Golden Hitler Youth Badge.

United We Stand

United we fall

Chapter 25

Jana Fielder had no idea what had happened to Dirk since that horrible night when he was dragged away by the Gestapo. Her husband had either been shot or was languishing in a Gestapo gaol.

The relationship with her son Wilhelm had become strained but always cordial as Jana couldn't afford to be on his wrong side or she could end up like Dirk.

Although an enthusiastic member of the BDM, Eva was also very wary of her brother who had demonstrated his fanatical commitment and support for the Fuhrer.

The war was not going well for Germany, most Germans now believed it was only a matter of time before capitulation.

1945

January 1-17 – Germans withdraw from the Ardennes.

January 16 – U.S. 1st and 3rd Armies link up after a month long separation during the Battle of the Bulge.

January 17 – Soviet troops capture Warsaw, Poland.

January 26 – Soviet troops liberate Auschwitz.

February 4-11 – Roosevelt, Churchill, and Stalin meet at Yalta.

February 13/14 – Dresden is destroyed by a firestorm after Allied bombing raids.

March 6 – Last German offensive of the war begins to defend oil fields in Hungary.

March 7 – Allies take Cologne and establish a bridge across the Rhine at Remagen.

March 30 – Soviet troops capture Danzig.

April – Allies discover stolen Nazi art and wealth hidden in German salt mines.

April 1 – U.S. troops encircle Germans in the Ruhr; Allied offensive in northern Italy.

April 12 – Allies liberate Buchenwald and Belsen concentration camps; President Roosevelt dies. Harry Truman becomes President.

April 16 – Soviet troops begin their final attack on Berlin; Americans enter Nuremberg.

April 18 – German forces in the Ruhr surrender.

April 21 – Soviets reach Berlin.

The Battle of Berlin, 1945

The final chapter in the destruction of Hitler's Third Reich began on April 16, 1945 when Stalin unleashed the brutal power of 20 armies, 6,300 tanks and 8,500 aircraft with the objective of crushing German resistance and capturing Berlin. By prior agreement, the Allied armies (positioned approximately 60 miles to the west) halted.

Their advance on the city stalled in order to give the Soviets a free hand. The depleted German forces put up a stiff defence, initially repelling the attacking Russians, but ultimately succumbed to overwhelming force. By April 24 the Soviet army surrounded the city, slowly tightening its stranglehold on the remaining Nazi defenders. Fighting street-to-street and house-to-house, Russian troops blasted their way towards Hitler's chancellery in the city's centre.

Inside his underground bunker Hitler lived in a world of fantasy as his "Thousand Year Reich" crumbled above him. In his final hours the Fuhrer married his long-time mistress and then joined her in suicide. The Third Reich was dead.

Beginning of the End

Dorothea von Schwanenfluegel was a twenty-nine-year-old wife and mother living in Berlin. She and her young daughter along with friends and neighbours huddled within their apartment building as the end neared. The city was already in ruins from Allied air raids, food was scarce, the situation desperate – the only hope that the Allies would arrive before the Russians. Here is Dorothea's account as the Russians begin the final push to victory:

"Friday, April 20, was Hitler's fifty-sixth birthday, and the Soviets sent him a birthday present in the form of an artillery barrage right into the heart of the city, while the Western Allies joined in with a massive air raid.

The radio announced that Hitler had come out of his safe bomb-proof bunker to talk with the fourteen to sixteen year old boys who had 'volunteered' for the 'honour' to be accepted into the SS and to die for their Fuhrer in the defence of Berlin. What a cruel lie! These boys did not volunteer, but had no choice, because boys who were found hiding were hanged as traitors by the SS as a warning that, 'he who was not brave enough to fight had to die.' When trees were not available, people were strung up on lamp posts. They were hanging everywhere, military and civilian, men and women, ordinary citizens who had been executed by a small group of fanatics. It appeared that the Nazis did not want the people to survive because a lost war, by their rationale, was obviously the fault of all of us. We had not sacrificed enough and therefore, we had forfeited our right to live, as only the government was without guilt. The Volkssturm was called up again, and this time, all boys age thirteen and up, had to report as our army was reduced now to little more than children filling the ranks as soldiers."

Encounter with a Young Soldier

"In honour of Hitler's birthday, we received an eight-day ration allowance, plus one tiny can of vegetables, a few ounces of sugar and a half-ounce of real coffee.

No one could afford to miss rations of this type and we stood in long lines at the grocery store patiently waiting to receive them. While standing there, we noticed a sad looking young boy across the street standing behind some bushes in a self-dug shallow trench. I went over to him and found a mere child in a uniform many sizes too large for him, with an anti-tank grenade lying beside him. Tears were running down his face, and he was obviously very frightened of everyone. I very softly asked him what he was doing there. He lost his distrust and told me that he had been ordered to lie in wait here, and when a Soviet tank approached he was to run under it and explode the grenade. I asked how that would work, but he didn't know. In fact, this frail child didn't even look capable of carrying such a grenade. It looked to me like a useless suicide assignment because the Soviets would shoot him on sight before he ever reached the tank.

By now, he was sobbing and muttering something, probably calling for his mother in despair, and there was nothing that I could do to help him. He was a picture of distress, created by our inhuman government. If I encouraged him to run away, he would be caught and hung by the SS, and if I gave him refuge in my home, the SS would shoot everyone in the house. So, all we could do was to give him something to eat and drink from our rations. When I looked for him early next morning he was gone and so was the grenade. Hopefully, his mother found him and would keep him in hiding during these last days of a lost war."

The Russians Arrive

"The Soviets battled the German soldiers and drafted civilians street by street until we could hear explosions and rifle fire right in our immediate vicinity. As the noise got closer, we could even hear the horrible guttural screaming of the Soviet soldiers, which sounded to us like enraged animals. Shots shattered our windows and shells exploded in our garden, and suddenly the Soviets were on our street. Shaken by the battle around us and numb with fear, we watched from behind the small cellar windows facing the street as the tanks and an endless convoy of troops rolled by...

It was a terrifying sight as they sat high upon their tanks with their rifles cocked, aiming at houses as they passed. The screaming, gun-wielding women were the worst. Half of the troops had only rags and tatters around their feet while others wore SS boots that had been looted from a conquered SS barrack in Lichterfelde. Several fleeing people had told us earlier that they kept watching different boots pass by their cellar windows. At night, the Germans in our army boots recaptured the street that the Soviets in the SS boots had taken during the day. The boots and the voices told them who was who. Now we saw them with our own eyes, and they belonged to the wild cohorts of the advancing Soviet troops.

Facing reality was ten times worse than just hearing about it. Throughout the night, we huddled together in mortal fear, not knowing what the morning might bring. Nevertheless, we noiselessly did sneak upstairs to double check that our heavy wooden window shutters were still intact and that all outside doors were barricaded. But as I peaked out, what did I see! The porter couple in the apartment house next to ours was standing in their front yard waving to the Soviets. So our suspicion that they were Communists had been right all along, but they must have been out of their minds to openly proclaim their brotherhood like that.

As could be expected, that night a horde of Soviet soldiers returned and stormed into their apartment house. Then we heard what sounded like a terrible orgy with women screaming for help, many shrieking at the same time. The racket gave me goose bumps. Some of the Soviets trampled through our garden and banged their rifle butts on our doors in an attempt to break in. Thank goodness our sturdy wooden doors withstood their efforts. Gripped in fear, we sat in stunned silence, hoping to give the impression that this was a vacant house, but hopelessly delivered into the clutches of the long-feared Red Army. Our nerves were in shreds."

Looting

"The next morning, we women proceeded to make ourselves look as unattractive as possible to the Soviets by smearing our faces with coal dust and covering our heads with old rags, our make-up for Ivan. We huddled together in the central part of the basement, shaking with fear, while some peeked through the low basement windows to see what was happening on the Soviet-controlled street. We felt paralysed by the sight of these husky Mongolians, looking wild and frightening. At the ruin across the street from us the first Soviet orders were posted, including a curfew. Suddenly there was a shattering noise outside. Horrified, we watched the Soviets demolish the corner grocery store and throw its contents, shelving and furniture out into the street. Urgently needed bags of flour, sugar and rice were split open and spilled their contents on the bare pavement, while Soviet soldiers stood guard with their rifles so that no one would dare to pick up any of the urgently needed food. This was just unbelievable. At night, a few desperate people tried to salvage some of the spilled food from the gutter. Hunger now became a major concern because our ration cards were worthless with no hope of any supplies.

Shortly thereafter, there was another commotion outside, even worse than before, and we rushed to our lookout to see that the Soviets had broken into the bank and were looting it. They came out yelling gleefully with their hands full of German bank notes and jewellery from safe deposit boxes that had been pried open. Thank God we had withdrawn money already and had it at home."

166

Surrender

"The next day, General Wilding, the commander of the German troops in Berlin, finally surrendered the entire city to the Soviet army. There was no radio or newspaper, so vans with loudspeakers drove through the streets ordering us to cease all resistance. Suddenly, the shooting and bombing stopped and the unreal silence meant that one ordeal was over for us and another was about to begin. Our nightmare had become a reality. The entire three hundred square miles of what was left of Berlin were now completely under control of the Red Army. The last days of savage house-to-house fighting and street battles had been a human slaughter, with no prisoners being taken on either side. These final days were hell. Our last remaining and exhausted troops, primarily children and old men, stumbled into imprisonment. We were a city in ruins; almost no house remained intact."

"The Battle of Berlin, 1945," Eye Witness to History,
www.eyewitnesstohistory.com (2002).

Jana was frightened for her children and herself. The SS had dictated that all Hitler Youth, boys and girls, report to the army headquarters for duty. They were to be the last line of defence against the Russian Red Army.

Wilhelm was an enthusiastic volunteer while Eva wasn't so keen but she knew to refuse would mean certain death. Berlin was in complete ruin, buildings destroyed, fires everywhere, and bodies hanging from lampposts.

Wilhelm arrived at the army base to see most of the boys from his battalion all dressed in army uniforms that looked three sizes too big, with helmets wobbling around on their fifteen year old heads. Upon receiving his own uniform Wilhelm was instructed to change immediately.

The boys were ordered into parade formation in the large quadrangle where they stood to attention for two hours. Three boys fainted and were taken away by the SS. Their fate was unknown although Wilhelm suspected they would be executed.

The SS Officer in charge strode to the front and addressed the now exhausted boys brigade.

'You are elite soldiers, Germany's finest who will repel the Russian hoards. It is your duty to give your lives, if necessary, to protect our beloved Fuhrer. You have trained for this mission since you joined the Hitler Youth. When we have defeated the filthy Russians the German people will laud you as heroes. Go do your duty.'

The boys were issued with Karabiner 98K rifles and grenades, commanded to march in formation behind an SS Officer. The officer, Captain Schmidt, assigned each boy a position along the route the Russians would take when entering the once great city of Berlin.

Wilhelm was directed to hold a bus shelter with instructions to fire on the tanks as they approached. When they were close enough he was to roll his grenades under the tank and shoot any Russians that tried to escape the vehicle. The order was to shoot anybody in the street as they should not be there and were probably Russian corroborators.

Wilhelm positioned himself behind the bus shelter, checked he had the full allocation of grenades and a fully loaded rifle magazine.

At 12 noon the streets of Berlin were deserted when he saw a woman endeavouring to cross the street. It appeared she was trying to retrieve a bag of fruit dropped by someone frantically racing for refuge away from the imminent street fight. Wilhelm took aim and fired at the woman. She dropped and remained motionless on the road. Orders were orders.

A Street in Berlin

Wilhelm felt no pity for the stupid woman, she knew the rules and chose to ignore them. At fifteen years of age Wilhelm had become a murderer, one of Hitler's boy assassins.

In the distance Wilhelm heard a muffled rumbling sound as Russian tanks approached central Berlin. It was another hour before he caught sight of the first tank, travelling slowly and firing its cannon into the odd building along its path.

Finally the tank reached the bus stop. Wilhelm grabbed a grenade from his belt, pulled the pin and ran forwards with the intention of rolling the explosive under the armoured vehicle. Having never used a grenade before he was under the impression it had a ten second fuse. However the type issued to the boys was five seconds. As he ran for the tank the grenade exploded in his hand tearing the teenager apart. The Russians on board the tank laughed out loud, 'Silly bastard'.

Wilhelm did not receive a burial.

Between twenty and thirty thousand Hitler Youth boys and girls died defending Berlin. Hitler dispatched children to the front line knowing there was little chance of them surviving the Russian onslaught.

Wilhelm's mother and sister survived the war and lived under Russian control until the Berlin Wall came down in July 1988. Jana was eighty-eight when she was finally able to visit her relatives in West Germany, Eva was fifty-nine.

Jana died in 1990.

Benedict Arnold

Boy Soldier

Chapter 25

Benedict Arnold

To comprehend the life of Benedict Arnold an understanding of American history is required. Benedict was just like the other boy soldiers described in this book, he was young, adventurous and foolish.

American History 1700 – 1763

1700 – The Anglo population in the English colonies in America reaches 275,000, with Boston as the largest city, followed by New York.

1700 – In June, Massachusetts passes a law ordering all Roman Catholic priests to leave the colony within three months, upon penalty of life imprisonment or execution. New York then passes a similar law.

1701 – July, The French establish a settlement at Detroit. In October, Yale College is founded in Connecticut.

1702 – March, Queen Anne ascends the English throne. In May, England declares war on France after the death of the King of Spain, Charles II, to stop the union of France and Spain. This War of the Spanish Succession is called Queen Anne's War in the colonies, where the English and American colonists will battle the French, their Native American allies, and the Spanish for the next eleven years.

1706 – January 17, Benjamin Franklin is born in Boston.

In November, South Carolina establishes the Anglican Church as its official church.

1711 – Hostilities break out between Native Americans and settlers in North Carolina after the massacre of settlers. The conflict, known as the Tuscarora Indian War will last two years.

1712 – May, the Carolina colony is officially divided into North Carolina and South Carolina.

In June, the Pennsylvania assembly bans the import of slaves into that colony.

In Massachusetts, the first sperm whale is captured at sea by an American from Nantucket.

1713 – Queen Anne's War ends with the Treaty of Utrecht.

1714 – Tea is introduced for the first time into the American Colonies. In August, King George I ascends to the English throne, succeeding Queen Anne.

1716 – The first group of black slaves is brought to the Louisiana territory.

1718 – New Orleans is founded by the French.

1720 – The population of American colonists reaches 475,000. Boston, 12,000 is the largest city, followed by Philadelphia, 10,000 and New York 7000.

1725 – The population of black slaves in the American colonies reaches 75,000.

1727 – King George II ascends the English throne.

1729 – Benjamin Franklin begins publishing The Pennsylvania Gazette, which eventually becomes the most popular colonial newspaper.

1730 – Baltimore is founded in the Maryland colony.

1731 – The first American public library is founded in Philadelphia by Benjamin Franklin.

1732 – February 22, George Washington is born in Virginia.

The first mass is celebrated in the only Catholic church in colonial America, Philadelphia.

In June, Georgia, the 13th English colony, is founded.

1732 – Benjamin Franklin publishes Poor Richard's Almanac selling nearly 10,000 copies per year.

1733 – The Molasses Act, passed by the English Parliament, imposes heavy duties on molasses, rum and sugar imported from non-British islands in the Caribbean to protect the English planters there from French and Dutch competition.

1734 – November, New York newspaper publisher John Peter Zenger is arrested and accused of seditious libel by the Governor.

In December, the Great Awakening religious revival movement begins in Massachusetts. The movement will last ten years and spread to all of the American colonies.

1735 – John Peter Zenger is brought to trial for seditious libel but is acquitted after his lawyer successfully convinces the jury that truth is a defence against libel.

1739 – England declares war on Spain. As a result, in America, hostilities break out between Florida Spaniards and Georgia and South Carolina colonists. Also in 1739, three separate violent uprisings by black slaves occur in South Carolina.

1740 – Fifty black slaves are hanged in Charleston, South Carolina, after plans for another revolt are revealed.

Europe, the War of the Austrian Succession begins after the death of Emperor Charles VI and eventually results in France and Spain allied against England. The conflict is known in the American colonies as King George's War and lasts until 1748.

1750 – The Iron Act is passed by the English Parliament, limiting the growth of the iron industry in the American colonies to protect the English Iron industry.

1751 – The Currency Act is passed by the English Parliament, banning the issuing of paper money by the New England colonies.

1754 – The French and Indian War erupts as a result of disputes over land in the Ohio River Valley. In May, George Washington leads a small group of American colonists to victory over the French, and then builds Fort Necessity in the Ohio territory. In July, after being attacked by numerically superior French forces, Washington surrenders the fort and retreats.

1755 – In February, English General Edward Braddock arrives in Virginia with two regiments of English troops. General Braddock assumes the post of commander in chief of all English forces in America. In April, General Braddock and Lieutenant Colonel George Washington set out with nearly 2000 men to battle the French in the Ohio territory.

In July, a force of about 900 French and Indians defeat those English forces. Braddock is mortally wounded. Massachusetts Governor William Shirley then becomes the new commander in chief.

1756 – England declares war on France, as the French and Indian War in the colonies now spreads to Europe.

1757 – In June, William Pitt becomes England's Secretary of State and escalates the French and Indian War in the colonies by establishing a policy of unlimited warfare. In July, Benjamin Franklin begins a five-year stay in London.

1758 – In July, a devastating defeat occurs for English forces at Lake George, New York, as nearly two thousand men are lost during a frontal attack against well-entrenched French forces at Fort Ticonderoga. French losses are 377. In November, the French abandon Fort Duquesne in the Ohio territory. Settlers then rush into the territory to establish homes. Also in 1758, the first Indian reservation in America is founded, in New Jersey, on 3000 acres.

1759 – French Fort Niagara is captured by the English. Also in 1759, war erupts between Cherokee Indians and southern colonists.

1759 – 13 September – The Fall of Quebec – Battle of the Plains of Abraham – British defeat French, thus gaining control of Canada.

1760 – The population of colonists in America reaches 1,500,000. In March, much of Boston is destroyed by a raging fire. In September, Quebec surrenders to the English.

In October, George III becomes the new English King.

1762 – England declares war on Spain, which had been planning to ally itself with France and Austria. The British then successfully attack Spanish outposts in the West Indies and Cuba.

1763 – The French and Indian War, known in Europe as the Seven Year's War, ends with the Treaty of Paris. Under the treaty, France gives England all French territory east of the Mississippi River, except New Orleans. The Spanish give up east and west Florida to the English in return for Cuba.

Benedict Arnold was born on January 14th, 1741 in Norwich, Connecticut. Only two of his mother's eleven children survived until adulthood – Benjamin was one of these. His mother had been a prosperous widow before marrying Benedict's father, a merchant. However, Benedict's father did not manage the family's money well and they were financially ruined by the time Benedict was thirteen. Benedict was forced to leave school and go to work learning to be an apothecary, a position similar to that of a modern-day pharmacist.

As a young man Benjamin Arnold was a risk-taker who looked for outlets for his energetic and impulsive nature, similar to other boys his age.

At sixteen years old he volunteered to fight with the British under the leadership of a young George Washington in the French and Indian War. He, along with many other young boys lied about their age to join in the heroic feats of their brothers and fathers.

It is reputed that at eighteen Benjamin deserted the army in order to be with his mother who was dying. In the 1760s he traded with Canada and the West Indies as a merchant and a sea captain. Taking his hot-headed nature to sea with him at least two duels were fought on trading voyages. Arnold was a financial success as a trader but was also accused of smuggling. In 1767 he married Margaret Mansfield, daughter of a government official in New Haven, Connecticut.

Also known as the Seven Years' War, this New World conflict marked another chapter in the long imperial struggle between Britain and France. When France's expansion into the Ohio River valley brought repeated conflict with the claims of the British colonies, a series of battles led to the official British declaration of war in 1756. Boosted by the financing of future Prime Minister William Pitt, the British turned the tide with victories at Louisbourg, Fort Frontenac and the French-Canadian stronghold of Quebec. At the 1763 peace conference, the British received the territories of Canada from France and Florida from Spain, opening the Mississippi Valley to westward expansion.

Benedict Arnold again raised arms in the American Revolutionary War and rose through the ranks to Brigadier General.

By 1780, Benedict was very bitter toward the Continental Congress. Appointed as the commander of the fort at West Point, New York, he offered to hand it over to British forces for a large sum of money. Arnold's plan, however, was discovered, and he quickly swore allegiance to the British. He commanded British forces in several small-scale battles, but Britain would soon back out of the war, much to his contempt.

Benedict Arnold, a boy soldier who became a successful military officer only to be regarded as America's greatest traitor.

An Uncivil War

Chapter 26

Causes of the American Civil War

It has long been assumed the Civil war occurred because the North was no longer willing to tolerate slavery as being part of the structure of U.S. society and that the political power brokers in Washington were planning to abolish slavery throughout the Union. Therefore for most people slavery is the fundamental issue in explaining the causes of the American Civil War

It's not quite that simple. Slavery was a major issue but not the only factor in pushing America into a horrendous bloody conflict.

By April 1861 the slavery issue had been entwined with other major issues such as state rights what these rights were is unclear. The southern states objected to the fact that the Federal Government was dictating what was wrong and what was right. They felt their whole way of life was changing for the worse and they didn't like it. The Southern States also didn't like the fact prior to the war about 75% of the money to operate the Federal Government was derived from the Southern States via an unfair sectional tariff on imported goods and the majority was from just four Southern States, Virginia, North Carolina, South Carolina and Georgia.

All these issues contributed to the American Civil War.

By 1860 America could not be seen as one society – the North and the South were like two separate countries each with their own value systems and interpretation of the rule of law.

It became North versus South, the Union versus the Confederates – and then WAR.

The Confederate States of America

South Carolina

Mississippi

Florida

Alabama

Georgia

Louisiana

Texas

Arkansas

North Carolina

Virginia

Tennessee

The Union States of America

California

Illinois

Iowa

Maine

Minnesota

New Hampshire

New Jersey

Oregon

Rhode Island

Wisconsin

Connecticut

Indiana

Kansas

Michigan

Nevada

New York

Ohio

Pennsylvania

Vermont

The South was agrarian; cotton and tobacco were the backbone of the region's economy with strong exports to markets in Western Europe.

The class structure in Britain was mimicked in the southern states. A local plantation owner was comparable to a Lord and the local population within his territory deferential towards such men.

The South constituted a strictly Christian society that had wealthy men at the top while those underneath were expected and required to accept their social status. Social advancement for the less privileged was possible but unusual. Invariably one advanced within the senior families, the economic, political and legal brokers of their state.

Certainly the wealth created by the plantation owners relied heavily on slave labour and was accepted, after all the first slaves arrived in Carolina in 1670. Therefore the south regarded slavery as the natural way of doing things. If slave labour was no longer available to work the plantations wealth of the landowners would have been seriously affected. It was not only the barons who would suffer but also the local communities that relied on their support.

When the dogs of war began to howl in 1860-61, many in the South saw their very way of life being threatened. Part of that was slavery, but it was not the only part.

The North's way of life was diametrically opposed to the South; it had become an industrial powerhouse with an economy growing at an incredible pace.

In the North you did not need to be born into a wealthy family; many poor boys became entrepreneurs such as Samuel Colt who died a multi-millionaire. Cornelius Vanderbilt was another example. Whether an immigrant from the Netherlands could have made his way into the social hierarchy of the South is highly unlikely.

The North was also a cosmopolitan mixture of nationalities and religions – far more so than the South. There can be little doubt that several important groups such as the Quakers and other religious organisations in the North were anti-slavery and wanted its abolition throughout the Union. However, there were also groups that were ambivalent and those who knew that the North's economic development was based not only on entrepreneurial skills but also on the input of poorly paid workers. While they had their freedom and were paid, their lifestyle was at best very harsh.

While the belligerents of the American Civil War were opposed in many areas, it became worse with the perception in the South that the North would try to impose its own values on their beloved land.

In 1832, South Carolina passed an act declaring Federal tariff legislation could not be enforced onto states. This meant after February 1st 1833 the tariffs would not be recognised in South Carolina. This brought the rogue state into direct conflict with the Federal government in Washington DC.

Congress passed the 'Force Bill' enabling the President to use military force to bring any state into line with regards to implementing Federal law. On this occasion the threat of military force worked, South Carolina capitulated.

It was at this time slavery became entwined with state rights. The question was, how much power was held by a state compared to Federal authority? The key issue was whether slavery would be allowed to continue in the newly created States joining the Union.

This dispute escalated when the federal government purchased Kansas. The new state was officially opened for settlement in 1854 when both pro- slavery and anti-slavery settlers poured in at the same time, establishing a scenario of violence and acrimony

South Carolina was the first state to secede from the Union on December 20th 1860. It felt it was being dominated by a Federal Government, which was controlled by the North. Whether this was true or not is irrelevant as many South Carolinians felt it to be the case.

The secession of South Carolina pushed other southern states into doing the same.

With such a background of distrust between most southern states and the Government in Washington, it only needed one incident to set off a civil war and that occurred at Fort Sumter in April 1861.

Fort Sumter

On Friday April 12th, 1861 the attack on Fort Sumter by the Confederate army began. This event is considered the beginning of the American Civil War.

In 1860, a Federal grant of $80,000 was given to complete the construction of Fort Sumter near Charleston South Carolina, as it had lain unfinished for a number of years.

The fort was constructed to hold a garrison of 650 men.

On April 12th 1861, General Beauregard of the Confederate forces attacked Fort Sumter. The fort housed three 10-inch guns placed to cover all the important angles. The fort also housed 8-inch columbiads 42lbs, 32lbs and 24lbs guns and some 8-inch sea howitzers. Fort Sumter had its own freshwater supply and a hospital.

All hell was about to break loose. More than 625,000 people would lose their lives, many of them children.

Union Columbiad

The fort was not fully manned when it was attacked but still held out until April 22nd after more than 40,000 shells had been fired at her.

By the end of the war in 1865, Fort Sumter was little more than a pile of rubble after constant shelling by Union forces.

Union Boys
v
Confederate Boys
Chapter 27

Ohio 1861

James Imlay, or Jimmy as his family called him, was a normal, athletic thirteen-year-old boy. The youngest of eight, he lived with his mother, father and brothers. His two eldest brothers, David and John, had married girls from the South and were living in Georgia and South Carolina.

Jimmy's hometown of Yellow Springs Ohio was a pretty spa town famous for its natural hot springs. Its history dated back over two hundred years. George Washington had commissioned a military hospital in the town after the revolutionary war.

Life was good for Jimmy, he attended the local school and had aspirations of becoming a teacher.

Ohio River 1861

Jimmy was aware of the rumblings of war, but like all his contemporaries hoped it wouldn't happen. His mother, Sarah, was more and more concerned about the tone of letters from her eldest boys David and John. It was clear they both felt strongly about the freedom of the South and were willing to place their lives on the line to defend the Confederacy.

Robert Imlay, Jimmy's father, felt just as strongly about the abolition of slavery.

Brother against brother, father against son, war was about to begin within the Imlay family and across the breadth of America.

In Cincinnati and surrounding towns like Yellow Springs hundreds of young men enlisted for military service; among them were Jimmy's brothers, Levi, George, William, Andrew, and Robert. Although their father Robert Snr was forty-six, he also enlisted to fight for this cause he so strongly believed in.

The only occupants left in the family home were Sarah and Jimmy; it felt strange and very quiet.

The Imlay men all joined the Ohio 3rd Regiment – at least they would be able to keep a protective eye out for each other.

Robert Snr, due to his age and experience was commissioned a Captain while the Levi was commissioned a Lieutenant. The younger boys were privates.

The first serious encounter the Imlays had with the Confederates took place at Beaver Creek Dam. This was the first of a number of battles called the Seven Day Battle.

The campaign took place from June 25 to July 1, 1862 and featured six different battles along the Virginia Peninsula east of Richmond. The Union Army of the Potomac, led by Major General George B. McClellan, was over 100,000 men strong. Yet a new field commander, General Robert E. Lee, shifted this sizeable group of Confederates from the ultimate goal of Richmond and back to the James River.

General Robert E. Lee

The Confederate President Jefferson Davis had appointed General Lee as a military adviser but when General Joseph E. Johnston was wounded during the Battle of Seven Pines, Davis asked Lee to take command of the army in the field. Lee immediately set the men to work building defensive positions around Richmond, leading his disgruntled soldiers to dub him "the Prince of Spades." Lee knew he could not protect the Confederate capital for long against such overwhelming odds. After General Thomas J. 'Stonewall' Jackson arrived with troops from the Shenandoah Valley Campaign, Lee prepared to strike McClellan's Union army.

However McClellan struck first, sending two divisions of the III Corps to secure the Richmond & York River Railroad. The intense fighting on June 25 in the swamps around Oak Grove proved indecisive.

The next day Lee took the initiative, assaulting Federal positions along Beaver Dam Creek, north of the Chickahominy River. The plan depended on a rapid movement by Jackson's weary troops, who arrived too late. Major General A. P. Hill's Confederate troops attacked as planned but were beaten back. However, the Federals, with Jackson on their right flank and Hill and Lieutenant General James Longstreet to their front and left, fell back behind Boatswain Creek east of Gaines Mill.

The casualties on both sides were mounting up. One of the Union soldiers killed was Levi Imlay.

On June 27, the Confederates attacked in a series of costly charges. On the south side of the Chicahominy, a Confederate force from Major General "Prince John" Magruder's command attacked Federals at Garnett's Farm but were repulsed. The savage attacks convinced the cautious McClellan that he needed to give up his plan to capture Richmond and fall back along his line of supply.

The 28th saw little fighting except for a failed Confederate reconnaissance attempt at Golding's Farm. On June 29, Magruder struck the Union rear guard at Savage's Station but with little effect.

On the 30th, three Confederate divisions hit Union positions in a battle known as Glendale or Frayser's Farm. The Union division of Brigadier General George A. McCall was routed and their commander was captured, but counterattacks stopped the Rebel advance. Farther north, an assault by Jackson stalled in White Oak Swamp, and to the south Federal gunboats turned a half-hearted attempt by Major General T. H. Holmes back.

McClellan took up a strong defensive position on Malvern Hill a little north of the James River. Lee hammered the defenders with repeated assaults that cost the Confederate army five thousand six hundred men but failed to take the position. Strategically, Lee had won. McClellan retreated down the peninsula. Richmond was saved.

Lee, whose reputation had previously suffered as a result of campaigns in Western Virginia over which he had little control, emerged as the Saviour of the South. By August, he had carried the fight back to Northern Virginia. The following month he would battle with McClellan again, this time along Antietam Creek outside Sharpsburg, Maryland.

Rebel Yell

Chapter 28

David Imlay managed a tobacco plantation, Magnolia for his father in-law Silas Veith. Employing five overseers and one hundred slaves, Veith produced some of the finest tobacco to come out of the South. David's views relating to slavery were diametrically opposed to those of his own father. This difference of opinion would ultimately lead to conflict in the true sense of the word.

The Veith family was regarded as one of the wealthiest families in Georgia. Silas Veith commanded respect from both politicians and other plantation owners. Even the slaves under his ownership respected Silas as a fair and even-handed master. Generals such as Robert E. Lee counted Silas Veith as a friend.

Silas and his wife Annette were blessed with six daughters, Charlotte, Sarah, Emma, Sophie, Anna and Mary and one son, Tom. The youngest child, Tom was only thirteen when war was declared between the North and South.

Silas and Annette were also proud grandparents to twenty grandchildren, all regularly visited and enjoyed the vast grounds of their plantation Magnolia.

When war began all their daughters' husbands, including David Imlay, volunteered.

David had moved south from Yellow Stone, leaving Ohio when he was seventeen, looking for adventure in what seemed at the time a far away place He worked on various cotton plantations before ending up at Magnolia. It was here, having worked his way up the plantation's hierarchy, he met Emma Veith. After a two-year romance the couple married and moved into one of the cottages on the Magnolia estate. David, albeit a northerner, soon adopted the philosophies of a southern gentleman – including the right to buy and sell slaves.

With the men of the family gone to war Silas was left with five overseers to run the plantation. Tom helped out after school and soon became a capable tobacco leaf classer.

Tom was as keen as his mother and sisters to hear news of the war and glorious battles against the Yankees. The young southerner dreamed of joining the fray and fighting alongside his southern brothers.

July 1863

Tom's birthday fell on the 4th of July. He would be turning fourteen.

This year his mother and sisters had organised a surprise birthday party. Their plan involved Tom returning from the tobacco-sorting shed to be surprised by his family and school friends waiting in the dining room. Tom normally arrived home at 4pm. Everybody waited in anticipation but when the clock struck 5pm his mother felt very concerned and went up to Tom's bedroom to see if he had somehow slipped into the house unnoticed.

Her son wasn't there but an envelope rested on his pillow addressed to her. Opening the envelope Annette Veith read the letter before beginning to cry and collapsing on the bed. Eventually the eldest daughter Charlotte came upstairs and found her distraught mother.

'What's wrong mother, why are you so upset?'

Annette handed the letter to Charlotte.

Dear Mother,

I am sorry to tell you this way but I knew if I told you face to face you'd try and stop me.

I'm volunteering to fight with the Confederate Army I know I'm doing the right thing for my self, my country and my family.

By the time you read this letter I'll be far away. I've changed my name so don't try and find me. With any luck I'll meet up with the boys.

I'm sorry I ruined my surprise party (Yes I Knew).

Say good-bye to my sisters and tell them I love them all.

Mum, I love you and would never want to hurt you but I know I'm doing the right thing.

All my love

Tom

'I must let father know. He'll be able to find Tom, he knows all the generals. Don't worry mother we'll fetch him back,' Charlotte said.

'You read the letter girl. He's changed his name. How on earth can we find him? There are probably hundreds if not thousands of young boys fighting.'

'Well there simply must be something we can do.'

Annette and Charlotte returned downstairs to the dining room and announced that the party had been cancelled as Tom had fallen ill. The last thing they wanted to do was announce Tom had run away to fight; not at that point in time anyway.

Silas Veith looked surprised. Tom had been perfectly well earlier that morning. Once all of Tom's friends had left Silas approached his wife.

'Annette what's going on? Tom seemed fine this morning.'

She passed Tom's letter to her husband, who read it and promptly slumped into his favourite armchair.

'You know we won't find him don't you?'

'Yes, I'm afraid I do.'

'I can ask around but I don't think it will do much good. They'll probably make him a drummer boy which won't necessarily keep him out of the firing line.'

The two distraught parents retired for the night although neither slept very much.

March to the Beat of a Different Drum

Chapter 29

Tom's Portrait

Tom Veith made his way to Atlanta by foot and train, arriving in the southern capital late at night. Not knowing where to go he found a safe place to sleep on a bench at the far end of the train platform. Finally Tom nodded off, only to be rudely woken around dawn by a Confederate captain.

> 'What do you think you're doing son? This is no place for a boy to be sleeping.'

'I'm sorry sir, I didn't have anywhere else to go.'

'Well, from the way you're dressed you don't look like a homeless boy. What's your story lad?'

'I've come to Atlanta to volunteer sir.'

'Have you now? How old are you?'

'Eighteen sir.'

'I don't think so boy, you don't look any older than sixteen to me.'

'I've always looked younger than my age sir.'

'I don't believe you son, however I admire your courage. Come with me and let's see if we can sort you out.'

Captain Norris led Tom out of the train station to a waiting carriage with a Confederate soldier at the reins. Once on board the officer ordered they be taken to the main barracks.

Tom was in awe. There were soldiers in grey everywhere, horses pulling gun carriages, rifles visible in wooden crates ready to be unloaded and allocated to newly recruited soldiers. It was a scene of frenetic activity.

Captain Norris guided Tom to the recruitment office where there were lines of young and not-so-young men waiting to be assessed.

Captain Norris approached the officer in charge and briefed him on his newfound recruit. The recruitment officer, ironically named Captain Grey, agreed to speak with the lad.

'Right boy, I believe you want to join the Confederate army?'

'Yes sir.'

'How old are you?'

'Eighteen sir.'

'Son you and I both know you are not eighteen. I can either send you back to your parents or I can accept you as a drummer boy. The choice is yours.'

'I don't know how to play a drum sir.'

'Don't worry, if we teach the older boys to shoot a rifle we can certainly teach you how to play a drum.'

'Well then, I'll join up as a drummer boy.'

'Excellent. Join the line for your medical and then we'll get you fitted out in uniform.'

Tom passed the medical immediately and was handed a uniform two sizes too large with a cap that covered his ears. True to Captain Grey's word Tom was allocated a drum and taught to play it correctly.

A drummer boy's recollection of the various beats and rolls were considered instrumental in the success of any campaign. During the cacophony of battle young Tom telegraphically communicated the officer's orders through his drum. He learned that one roll meant 'attack immediately' while another critical order was the drumroll instructing soldiers to retreat.

The most frightening roll for the enemy to hear was the long roll – the signal to attack along the entire front. The first drummer would begin alerting other drummers in earshot to also start playing the long roll. Eventually all the drummers would be simultaneously playing the long roll beat; a loud frightening symphony of death for the enemy.

Tom quickly picked up drumming and the various connotations of the beat, soon ready to join the battle against the hated Yankees.

Yellow Springs Ohio (Union) July 1963 - Union

Jimmy Imlay was not enjoying being the only male in the household. He loved his mother very much and felt a sense of responsibility for her safety in such turbulent times. But he also believed he should contribute to the war effort against the South. Jimmy was aware of several boys his age who had run away to join the Yankee army and thought he really should do the same. He dreamed of finding his father and brothers fighting the southern rebels with his brothers in arms.

After this idea played on his mind for months he finally decided to go. Late one night he wrote a letter to his mother and slipped out of the bedroom window. Jimmy headed south to Cincinnati and eventual glory.

Dear Mother,

Don't be angry, don't be sad. I've left to join the Union army and hopefully fight beside Dad and the boys. I feel like it is my duty as a man to do this. I'll write to you when I've settled into army life.

Your loving son,

Jimmy

Jimmy's First Drumming Lesson

Jimmy made his way to the main army barracks in Cincinnati and joined the line of volunteers ready to give their lives for the cause. When it was his turn to approach the large desk and two recruitment officers he tried to look as straight and tall as possible.

'Name?'

'Jimmy Smith sir.'

'Age?'

'Eighteen sir.'

The officer looked up from his paperwork and began to chuckle.

'Eighteen eh?'

'Yes sir, last birthday.'

'Really?'

'Yes sir.'

'What do you think Lieutenant? Do you think this boy is eighteen?'

'I'd say more like fifteen or sixteen Captain.'

'Son I think we all know you're not eighteen, not even seventeen, but we need lads like you in this army. We'll sign you up as a drummer boy and let's see where it leads you. Alright?'

'Yes sir thank you sir.'

Jimmy was soon fitted for a uniform and received extensive training on rolls, beats, and codes. After four weeks he was assigned to the 4th Ohio Regiment.

His first taste of war would be at Chickamauga.

Chickamauga

Let the Drumming Begin

Chapter 30

September 1863

The Battle of Chickamauga in Georgia saw General Braxton Bragg's army of Tennessee defeat a Union force commanded by General William Rosecrans.

Earlier in the month after Rosecrans' troops pushed the Confederates out of Chattanooga, Bragg had called for reinforcements and launched a counterattack on the banks of nearby Chickamauga Creek. After two days of battle and heavy losses on both sides the Southern rebels forced Rosecrans' Union soldiers to retreat.

Bragg failed to take advantage of the victory allowing the Federals to safely reach Chattanooga.

Ulysses S. Grant soon arrived with additional soldiers and that November the Federals reversed the results of Chickamauga and scored a victory in the region.

September 19th 1863

Jimmy was sitting on the damp ground, drum beside him, ready to go into battle. With him were five other drummer boys between twelve and seventeen years old. The early morning mist created an ethereal and haunting atmosphere, the calm before the firestorm of battle.

Chattanooga at Dawn

Captain Pierce approached them.

> 'OK lads, we're close to engaging the enemy. Drums ready and follow me.'

The six nervous boys followed the captain to where General Rosecrans was assembling his troops. Thousands of Union soldiers stood in a formation stretching back far further than Jimmy could see.

The Rebels' drums could be heard in the distance – a haunting sound that drifted across the meadows.

They could just make out grey figures emerging from the mist, the beat of drumsticks on pigskin, the sound of boots on the ground getting louder and louder.

General Bragg gave the order and the Confederates ran forward to confront the Blue Coats. Shots were fired, as was canon. Jimmy was ordered to drum the 'move forward' signal setting the Federals in motion towards the Grey Coats.

The battle of Chickamauga had begun.

Jimmy and the other drummer boys were having trouble keeping up with their battalion. The pace was furious until the two armies confronted each other – a mere hundred yards separating them. Then the dynamics changed.

Jimmy pounded the pigskin, giving his utmost to the drum so it would be heard over the gunfire and screaming. All around him soldiers were falling. Others took their place; many of these toppled with horrendous wounds or were dead before they hit the ground.

General Rosecrans rode his white stallion up and down the Union lines shouting orders to his troops. Smoke from the rifles and cannon fire created a thick haze making it difficult for either side to determine who was winning this battle.

'Hey Jimmy, are you all right?' shouted his new pal Billy.

'Bloody hell Billy I knew things would be bad but this is crazy.'

'I'm not sure what we're meant to be drumming. I haven't seen an officer to instruct us for ages. Well, not one that's alive.'

Just then a Union captain rode up and yelled for the two boys to begin drumming the retreat roll. Banging their drums as loud as possible the other drums in the distance started up soon the Federal army began its retreat to Chattanooga.

The Rebels weren't making it easy for the defeated Union soldiers, continuing to fire and running after the blue coats until the Union troops crossed the Tennessee River.

Jimmy was fording the river when a Confederate soldier fired his rifle. The Rebel wasn't aiming at a particular target, more of a 'don't come back now' shot at the retreating Federal troops.

Jimmy felt a burning pain between his shoulder blades dropped into the river and died. It didn't really matter whether it was the bullet or drowning that killed Jimmy. This young boy was another victim of man's inability to solve differences through negotiation rather than war.

Chattanooga: The Confederate Perspective

General Braxton Bragg decided not to pursue the Union army further than the river and was widely criticised by his subordinate generals, including Longstreet and Forrest, for not finishing the job.

Though Longstreet and his fellow general Forrest encouraged pursuit of the enemy the following morning, Bragg was preoccupied with the toll taken on his army from the battle at Chickamauga. Ten Confederate generals had been killed or wounded and overall Confederate casualties numbered close to 20,000. The Union suffered some 16,000 casualties, making the Battle of Chickamauga the costliest one in the war's western theatre.

Bragg's inaction turned a tactical triumph for the South into a strategic defeat, as Union forces were allowed to get safely to Chattanooga. Subsequently the Confederates put that city under siege but in October General Ulysses S. Grant arrived with reinforcements taking over Union command in the region. In November, Grant's forces reversed the results of Chickamauga with a decisive victory over the Confederates in the Battle of Chattanooga

Young Tom the drummer boy survived the battle and helped bury his dead comrades the following day. It was confronting for such a young boy to see such horrible carnage. A day that would never be forgotten.

Aftermath of the Battle

Tom went on to become a regular soldier carrying a rifle rather than a drum. After surviving many battles he returned home in 1865 – no longer a boy.

Abraham Lincoln

Four score and seven years ago our fathers brought forth on this continent a new nation, conceived in liberty, and dedicated to the proposition that all men are created equal.

Now we are engaged in a great civil war, testing whether that nation, or any nation so conceived and so dedicated, can long endure. We are met on a great battlefield of that war. We have come to dedicate a portion of that field, as a final resting place for those who here gave their lives that that nation might live. It is altogether fitting and proper that we should do this.

But, in a larger sense, we cannot dedicate, we cannot consecrate, we cannot hallow this ground. The brave men, living and dead, who struggled here, have consecrated it, far above our poor power to add or detract. The world will little note, nor long remember what we say here, but it can never forget what they did here. It is for us the living, rather, to be dedicated here to the unfinished work which they who fought here have thus far so nobly advanced. It is rather for us to be here dedicated to the great task remaining before us—that from these honoured dead we take increased devotion to that cause for which they gave the last full measure of devotion—that we here highly resolve that these dead shall not have died in vain—that this nation, under God, shall have a new birth of freedom—and that government of the people, by the people, for the people, shall not perish from the earth.

Abraham Lincoln – November 19, 1863.

African Conflict

Chapter 31

Uganda Africa 1989

Isaac Brungi was a typical Ugandan boy of eleven. Most days he played soccer with his friends on the dirt road outside his parents' house. Isaac aspired to become another Pele or Beckham and eventually live in a big house in the capital Kampala or even Hollywood.

The other boys regarded Isaac as the village's best player and he knew that with hard work on his game he just might make his dream come true.

Grace, Isaac's big sister, wasn't interested in soccer. She was focused on school and study with the ambition of becoming a doctor. Elijah and Peace, Isaac and Grace's parents, both worked a small farm holding incorporating cattle and goats. The additional crops of wheat and corn meant the farm provided for the family and fed them adequately.

Elijah and Peace had survived the tumultuous years when Idi Amin ruled Uganda.

In 1971, General Idi Amin overthrew the elected government of Milton Obote, declared himself president of Uganda and launched a ruthless eight-year regime during which an estimated 300,000 civilians were massacred. By expelling all Indian and Pakistani citizens in 1972 and simultaneously increasing military expenditure, Idi Amin triggered a massive economic decline for Uganda, the impact of which lasted for decades.

His reign of terror ended in 1979 when Ugandan exiles and Tanzanians took control of Kampala, forcing Amin to flee the capital. Never brought to justice for his heinous crimes, Idi Amin lived out the remainder of his life in Saudi Arabia.

General Idi Amin

Elijah, Isaac's father, was born the year Idi Amin came into power and despite only being eight years old when the tyrant was deposed every aspect of his life greatly affected by this evil despot. Both Elijah's parents had been murdered by Amin's troops and his grandmother raised him in the village of Nambale. The Brungi family lived in the same village and house as where Elijah grew up.

Life was never easy in Uganda but at least they could live in relative safety without the fear of being murdered in their sleep by the murderous henchmen of Amin.

Uganda 1985

Things changed when the 'The Lord's Resistance Army' began life in the early 1980s as the Holy Spirit Movement, led by a woman called Alice Lakwena, who claimed the Holy Spirit had ordered her to overthrow the Ugandan government which was accused of treating her people, the Acholi tribe of the North unfairly. As resentment towards the Ugandan government intensified, supporters flocked to Lakwena, and the Holy Spirit movement gathered momentum, until a battle won by the government led to Lakwena's exile.

Alice Lakwena

With no clear direction for the movement, a man claiming to be Lakwena's cousin, Joseph Kony, took over as leader and rebranded the movement in 1986 as the Lord's Resistance Army (LRA). Kony initially stated that the LRA's mission was to overthrow the government and rule Uganda based on the Ten Commandments. Rapidly losing support and in frustration Kony began abducting thousands of children to swell its ranks, turning them into killers and unleashing them on villages throughout Uganda.

Joseph Kony

Demonising the Innocents

Chapter 32

Nambale Uganda 1990

The village of Nambale has a population of 500 it is located close to the shores of Lake Victoria and is 111 kilometres from Uganda's capital Kampala.

It was Sunday morning; the routine for the Brungi family was to attend church at the village chapel before returning home when Grace and Peace would prepare Sunday lunch. The entire family enjoyed Sundays, it was their one day off from the normal farm duties and lunch was the highlight of the week.

The minister was in the middle of his sermon espousing the virtues of honesty and hard work when the doors of the chapel were flung open. About twenty LRA rebels burst through brandishing AK47 rifles and machetes. The leader strode up to the pulpit and slashed the minister's throat, almost decapitating him.

The other rebels began separating the children from their parents and elders, all the while shouting LRA slogans. Once the children were gathered the rest of the congregation was slaughtered. The terrified youngsters had been warned not to cry or show any emotion unless they wanted to be killed. After being dragged outside, the terrified children were roped together ready for the long trek back to the LRA camp.

Speaking was forbidden but despite the threat of severe punishment a young boy, no more than twelve years old, broke the rule. A soldier severed the boy's bottom lip, promising to sever the top lip if another word was spoken. A dirty rag was given to stem the bleeding and the injured boy ordered back in line to continue marching.

Isaac and his sister Grace were in total shock after witnessing their beloved parents be hacked to death. Now they were being marched to an unknown destination. What was to be their fate?

After about four hours the group arrived at a series of grass huts enclosed in a corral, the LRA camp. Pushed to the ground the children were again warned about talking.

Isaac in the LRA Camp

Grace's Story

'Once Isaac and I arrived at the LRA camp they separated all the girls from the boys. I with about twenty other girls was kept in a hut meant for ten. I knew all the girls. Some were my friends. We were ordered not to converse. We all saw what happened to the young boy on the march getting his lip severed so we obeyed although we did try and communicate through hand signals. It's amazing how you can communicate with your hands and your facial expressions. A guard threw a couple of loaves of bread and a half eaten chicken into the hut. It was like Jesus and the loaves and fishes, we all got a share but they were tiny portions. That evening several soldiers arrived and pointed at several of the girls including me. We were instructed to follow them to the outer edge of the camp where the jungle was thick. That was the first time I was brutally raped. It was not how I pictured I would lose my virginity.

For the next six years I was in captivity – a sex slave and a mule carrying ammunition and other supplies through the bush. There was very little food to eat.

The last time I saw my brother Isaac was that horrific night after our parents were killed in chapel.

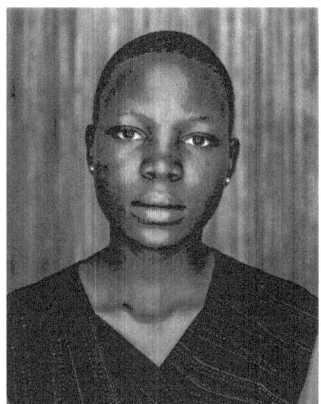

Grace Aged 20

The Ugandan army liberated me after a fierce battle with the LRA. Of the twenty girls who were kidnapped with me six years earlier, only five of us remained. The others died from disease or ill treatment, several hacked to death after trying to escape.

The soldiers returned me to my village of Nambale to find another family living in my family home where my father grew up. Even after I'd explained that the house belonged to my family they just laughed and called me an LRA whore. I went to the village chief but he was not prepared to help saying possession is nine-tenths of the law.

Eventually I found a family that was willing to take me in and I returned to school. After three years I passed my secondary school diploma and am now training to become a nurse.'

Isaac's Story

'When we arrived at the camp, the LRA soldiers led all the girls away. That was the last time I saw my sister Grace during the eight years I was with the LRA.

The soldiers ordered ten or so boys to follow them into the bush they lined us up. The leader approached each boy with a bunch of small sticks in his hand and told us to choose one. After each boy had chosen a stick the LRA leader examined them. The boy with the shortest stick was ordered to stand in front of the group.

The remaining boys were issued with machetes and ordered to hack this poor boy to death. Anyone who refused would be killed by one of the soldiers. We had no choice. We were terrified but all slashed at him until he stopped screaming. He was dead; I had just committed my first murder. This was our first training session on how to kill. Eventually, we would do so without emotion.

Over the following eight years I committed many more murders, all under the orders of the LRA.

The boys from my village became an integral part of the LRA army quicker than the other soldiers and paid less. We also obeyed orders without question.

My comrades and I would enter a village and round up all the adults to shoot or machete, killing them in front of their children. After stealing anything of worth, including provisions like food we would lead those children away to become child warriors like us.'

The LRA's recipe for making killers of children had three ingredients. First, abandon all hope of returning home. Next they must be blooded by the act of a murder. Finally, through superstition and ritual, their new persona would be inflated with their own sense of esteem. Underpinning all this, though, there's a final constant: rage.

Rage at their beatings and starvation; at the atrocities they're witnessing; at the crimes they were now committing.

More than anything else when Isaac recounts his story he talks of his own possession, not by the spirits but by the furies.

'Whenever I saw anything, it was not with a good heart. All my mind was full of destruction.'

'One day a friend from my village, Joseph who had been abducted at the same time as me whispered that we needed to talk. We arranged to meet on the outskirts of the camp. This was very dangerous, if we had been caught the soldiers would have killed us.'

'Isaac, I've heard that the Ugandan army is closing in on our camp. I think we should try and escape and find them. This will be our only hope of retuning to our village and hopefully begin leading a normal life.'

'You know what they'll do to us if we're caught don't you?'

'I know but I think it's worth a try. I can't stand killing our people anymore. When I saw them throwing babies into the fire during last week's raid, well I knew I had to escape.'

The two boys decided to make a run for it then and entered the jungle, hacking a path with their machetes. After about three hours, exhausted they made a bed from palm leaves and rested. Isaac was startled awake by the sound of voices, expecting to see LRA soldiers. To his vast relief it was four members of the Ugandan army who had discovered them.

Joseph and Isaac were led away for questioning and after a week transferred to a 'Treatment Centre' in Gulu.

Isaac and Joseph were reprogrammed at the centre for eighteen months and then allowed to return to their village – at last brother and sister were reunited.

Eventually the people of Nambale accepted them and both men married and began raising a family.

Isaac would never stop having nightmares reliving his murderous days with Kony's misfit army.

At last the people of Uganda could look forward to some sort of future and the children could become children again.

Boko Haram

Chapter 33

What is Boko Haram?

Boko Haram is a militant group in north-eastern Nigeria whose real name is actually 'Jama'at Ahl al-Sunna li al-Da'awat wa al-Jihad' which means Sunni Group for Preaching and Jihad. The group was founded in 2002, largely to preach an Islamist ideology based on the doctrines of the Taliban as well as groups such as al-Qaeda. It sought to disassociate itself from the Nigerian state and form a community only of its followers.

Wikipedia

Having virtually seceded from Nigeria, the leaders of Boko Haram knew that armed confrontation with the Nigerian Government was inevitable.

In 2009 the civil war began in earnest. During a major battle Boko Haram's founder, Mohammed Yusuf, was captured and died in police custody. The group continued to target Christian communities in north-eastern Nigeria and traditional Muslim leaders who objected to the group's violent tactics or ideology of the new leader, Abubakar Shekau.

The Islamic warlord ascribes to a Takfirist ideology; he labels other people as infidels and believes this justifies violent treatment of all others.

Abubakar Shekau has emerged since he became leader in 2002 as the face of Boko Haram, representing the group in its videos and statements.

He continues to threaten the Nigerian president and entire population of Nigeria, plus warn Western countries ranging from the US, UK, and France, extending his menace towards the United Nations too.

There are various assertions that Boko Haram is linked to al-Qaeda. However al-Qaeda has never formally recognised Boko Haram as an affiliate as was done with al-Qaeda in the Islamic Maghreb (AQIM) or al-Shabaab in Somalia. Nonetheless the operational linkages between higher-level Boko Haram members and the al-Qaeda network are very clear. Many Major Boko Haram attacks appear to have been led by Nigerians who trained with various al-Qaeda groups.

Boko Haram has also become affiliated with ISIS.

ISIS welcomed a pledge of allegiance made to it by Boko Haram and vowed to press with its expansion.

"We announce to you to the good news of the expansion of the caliphate to west Africa because the caliph … has accepted the allegiance of our brothers of the Sunni group for preaching and the jihad." claimed an ISIS leader.

Izghe, Northern Nigeria 2013

Cricket was introduced to Nigeria by the British in the late 19th century and became a national sporting obsession.

Benjamin was playing cricket on the dirt street running through his village of Izghe. The boys playing with him were all about the same age, twelve. They couldn't manage two teams of eleven so they made do with six players a side.

His best friend Victor was bowling while Ben was wicket keeping, they made a formidable pair. Benjamin's team won the game, which was as expected. There were no surprises in the result due to the fact Ben, being the eldest, always picked the best players for his team.

When they finished the game night was beginning to fall and the boys returned to their homes where the women of the household were preparing dinner.

Benjamin lived in a rudimentary shack with his mother, father, two younger brothers, Sam and Jacob and his older sister Rose. His grandmother also lived with the family group.

While the family sat around the table eating their tuwo masara, a traditional Nigerian corn flour dish, conversation moved to discussing young Benjamin. His father, Joseph announced that Ben would be spending some time with his brother's family in Maiduguri to learn the art of silversmithing, a highly respected profession. At first, Ben was not keen, it meant time away from his family and friends. When his father explained how this profession would improve his quality of life, give him an income, and help support his family, Benjamin warmed to the idea.

The day came for Benjamin to move to Maiduguri. Many villagers came out to wave goodbye and wish him good luck. The saddest person was Victor. They had been born two days apart and had always been best friends. Benjamin too was sad to say farewell to his buddy.

The truck heading for Maiduguri was also carting cattle and produce to be sold at market. Benjamin crammed into the front seat with the driver and co-driver. The roads were not particularly good making the trip uncomfortable.

Finally they arrived in the city. Benjamin was amazed, less than 200 people in his village of Izghe, Maiduguri had a population of over half a million. There were people everywhere plus cars and motorbikes zooming along the streets. This was all very foreign to the young lad having never even seen a motorbike before.

His uncle Emmanuel met him at the truck depot and took Ben home to meet the rest of the family. The house was constructed with mud bricks and had many rooms, nothing like his the shack back in the village. Emmanuel showed Benjamin his room. Ben couldn't believe he would have his own room. Back home only his mother and father had a separate bedroom. Ben began to understand some of what his father had said about working hard. This was the direction that should be taken if he was going to enjoy a comfortable future.

The following day Ben began his apprenticeship. The novice silversmith couldn't have predicted how his life would change forever.

A Stolen Childhood

Chapter 34

Victor was once again playing cricket in the dirt street of his village of Izghe. Although his love for the game hadn't diminished it wasn't quite the same without Benjamin wicket keeping. The win loss ratio had altered considerably now that Ben wasn't captaining the team.

The light was beginning to fade and the boys decided to end the match. They were picking up the fruit boxes they used as stumps when they heard the sound of trucks coming their way. The village didn't receive much traffic, so a convoy of trucks was an unusual event.

Six troop carriers rolled into the village. The boys, who had been enjoying their cricket game five minutes earlier, now stood by the side of the road watching in awe, bat and ball discarded on the ground.

Soldiers of Boko Haram alighted from the truck and began yelling orders to the villagers.

> 'Everybody come out of your houses and assemble in the street. All the men go to the far end of the village and await our orders. Women and children assemble at the opposite end. We are the liberators, we are Boko Haram. We are the protectors of the Prophet. You are Christians and don't deserve to live.'

The leader of the group approached the women and children looking for boys he could recruit as soldiers and girls who would become sex slaves.

Next, the Boko Haram terrorists searched every house. Anybody they found hiding was murdered. Once the leader was convinced all the villagers were assembled he ordered his troops to murder the men and any boys that weren't selected as recruits. The terrorists either shot them or hacked them to death.

Victor had two younger brothers, Charles aged 7 and James aged 5. They were killed along with the men, the terrorists dismissed them as too young to be useful. Victor's grandmother hid under her bed, she was found and hacked to death with a machete.

Victor was one of the boys selected. He was loaded into a truck and taken away to the Boko Haram camp over 150 kilometres away, hidden in dense bushland. His childhood of school, cricket and his belief in Jesus had just ended.

The trucks pulled up outside what looked like a jungle fort. Victor and the other boys were ordered to alight the truck, and marched to a compound. This was also where the boys kidnapped before them were housed.

Over the coming weeks the new boys were beaten and forced to attend executions, all in the name of Allah. They also attended classes conducted by the group's religious leader. If they were to become Boko Haram warriors they must convert to Islam; if they refused they were killed.

Three months passed since the time of their capture when Masud, the leader of the group, gathered the boys together, announced they were now officially Boko Haram soldiers and it was time to fight the infidel.

Three trucks pulled up. The young warriors were ordered to climb aboard and their mentors, all seasoned terrorists, followed behind them. Their objective was Sokoto, a village of three hundred Christians.

Victor and Comrades

The journey took three hours, the trucks rolled into Sokoto at six in the evening.

'Everybody out, round up all the infidels into the village square. If anyone resists shoot them,' shouted Masud.

The scene was bedlam, people were running away and being shot. Victor shot his first victim, the first of many.

Finally the square was crowded with villagers and Boko Haram terrorists. Masud ordered the men and boys be separated from the woman and girls. The soldiers then slaughtered the men and the boys who they deemed not suitable for recruitment. They chose girls that would suit their purposes aged between 10 and 16. They allowed the remaining women all too old to return to their houses.

Victor was proud of the way he conducted himself, a boy warrior.

Victor became a regular in Boko Haram, participating in regular raids and enjoying the raping of any young girls they captured. Any semblance of the young boy playing cricket and attending school was long gone.

Benjamin was sitting cross-legged in his uncle's workshop beating a silver pot into shape. Seemingly he had a natural aptitude for silversmithing and his progress had impressed his uncle Emmanuel who was giving Ben increasingly intricate pieces to work on.

It was near the end of the day and Benjamin was looking forward to the evening meal. His auntie Ruth was an excellent cook, using ingredients from their garden as well as the odd goat or lamb from the small stock holding

Ben left the workshop and walked the short distance to the house. Loud conversation and laughter could typically be heard emanating from the kitchen area where they all ate. Tonight there was only a deathly silence.

His auntie, uncle and two cousins were sitting at the table.

'Why the sad faces everybody?'

'Sit down Benjamin. I'm afraid we have some terrible news.'

Benjamin knew he didn't want to hear what was about to be said. He looked at his uncle.

Emmanuel disclosed the shocking news from Izghe. Now it was his Mother and himself left.

Benjamin quickly left the room and entered his bedroom, lying on the bed and crying uncontrollably for what seemed hours.

The family invited Benjamin's mother to come and stay with them rather than live alone with the horrible memories. She finally accepted after some persuasion.

Benjamin worked the next day and although his mood was understandably sombre he was just as diligent as normal.

But as the days passed into weeks and the weeks into months Benjamin's auntie and uncle became more and more concerned about his mental state. Benjamin spent most of his free time in his room not interacting with the rest of his family.

One morning Benjamin didn't arrive at work as normal. Emmanuel waited an hour and then went home to see if Benjamin was unwell. Entering the boy's room a note was found on the bed.

Dear Auntie Ruth and Uncle Emmanuel,

I am joining the JTF (The Civilian Joint Task Force).

I want to get the people who killed my family

Love

Benjamin

A similar letter was left for his Mother.

Payback

Chapter 35

It didn't take Benjamin long to find the training base for the Civilian Joint Task Force (JTF).

Benjamin approached a soldier wearing the familiar light blue uniform of the JTF and requested information about enlisting in the civilian force. He was directed to a building at the far end of the parade ground.

Recruits Reading Oath of Allegiance

A captain of the JTF interviewed Benjamin. Once his story was told the captain had no hesitation inviting Benjamin to join the people's militia.

After receiving basic training the young recruit was issued with the light blue uniform and a M16 semi automatic rifle.

Benjamin was involved in a number of battles with Boko Haram and proving his worth as a soldier.

December 2014

Gumsuri, Northern Nigeria

It was a day like any other day in the small village of Gumsuri. Women were washing clothes, men were attending their vegetable gardens and children were playing in the street.

The noise of trucks approaching alerted the villagers. They knew the reputation of Boko Haram and the devastation they would bring.

Then again it could be the JTF searching for the terrorists, a much better alternative. Unfortunately for them it was the former.

Six pickups drove into the village and about fifty Boko Haram militants disembarked and started rounding up all the women and children in one area and the men and boys in another.

Victor was part of the group guarding the men and boys. Once suitable recruits were selected Victor and his comrades slaughtered the men where they stood.

The women and children were all bound and marched out of Gumsuri. The boys who had been spared were loaded onto the pickups and driven to the local Boko Haram camp.

It took two days for word to reach Maiduguri, as the communication tower in Gumsuri had been destroyed during the raid. A villager who had escaped brought the news of the massacre.

The JTF responded immediately, determined to free the kidnapped women and children. More than a hundred JTF soldiers including Benjamin set out in a convoy of trucks to hunt down the terrorists and hopefully bring them to justice. According to the JTF, justice for Boko Haram was a bullet to the head.

After travelling a hundred kilometres to Gumsuri the convoy found only unspeakable horror. The civilian army group buried the dead and searched futilely for any survivors from the attack.

The group began tracking the guerrillas, a skill many of them were expert at.

After three days they came across the Boko Haram camp. Peering through the bush they could see women and girls contained in a large corral with a shed at one end.

Boko Haram soldiers were walking around or sitting in a circle smoking and laughing. The JTF commanding officer, David James signalled to his men to attack, one hundred JTF troops firing their weapons caught the rebels by surprise; they were soon captured or shot. One hour later they had been defeated and the kidnapped women and children released.

Benjamin scoured the camp making sure there were no wounded. To his dismay he discovered the body of Victor, his best friend. Benjamin fell to his knees and hugged the lifeless body.

Victor was only fourteen... just a boy.

Suicide Boy

I.S. Graduate

Chapter 36

October 2014

Akram Elazar lived in the Syrian village of Salma in northwestern Syria, located northeast of Latakia. Nearby localities include Mashqita and Ayn al-Bayda to the west, al-Haffah to the southwest, Aramo and Slinfah 12 km to the south, and Kinsabba to the north.

Salma means *peaceful, righteous, honest*. At fourteen Akram was like all normal Syrian teenagers, playing soccer, watching Kung Fu movies and listening to music on his iPod.

Akram was one of the brightest kids in his class, his ambition was to study medicine at university and become a doctor.

Well, that was the plan.

Akram was a dedicated Sunni Muslim, attending Friday prayers without failure.

One Friday, at the village mosque, two men approached him.

'Akram, we would like a word with you.'

'What about? I have to be home soon and help my Father milk the goats.'

'This won't take long, but is extremely important. It's about your dedication to Islam.'

Mohammed, Ayman and Akram walked to a café, ordered coffee and sat at a table at the very back of the establishment.

'Akram, are you aware that Shiites are murdering our men and boys and raping our women every day?' asked Mohammed.

'No, but I'm not surprised, the stinking infidels.'

'We want you to help us rid our land of these non-believers Akram,' said Ayman.

'How can I do that?'

'You can join the holy warriors Islamic State. We are the only true Muslims who actually practice Islam as the Prophet preached.'

'What do I need to do?'

'Come with us now and we will teach you all the things you need to know. God willing you may become a martyr.'

'I'll have to go home and get my parents' permission first.'

'There's no time for that. We will let your parents know where you are. They will be so proud of you Akram.'

Mohammed, Ayman and Akram left the café and walked back to the mosque where their utility was parked. Akram's life was about to change forever.

That day the two ISIS recruiters and the innocent young boy drove across the Iraq border to Mosul. Mosul, an oil-rich city, had been captured the previous year and was now an ISIS stronghold.

ISIS had established training centres around Mosul to enable the children they had recruited to be taught all things military and religious. Indoctrination was their goal, ensuring an endless supply of ISIS warriors.

The children, known as 'cubs of the caliphate' were trained in various disciplines including physical fitness, reciting the Quran and marksmanship. Their trainers continually emphasised the need to kill the 'hate-filled Shiites'.

Akram had been a member of ISIS for a month when he and his fellow recruits were assembled in a large hall. The group leader addressed everyone on the importance of being a Muslim warrior and how the infidel must be destroyed. His greatest tirade was naturally about the Shiites.

The ISIS leader gave the boys a choice; become foot soldiers or volunteer as a suicide bomber.

Akram had become despondent with ISIS, the public beheadings and other atrocities were proving too much. Back in his village severe punishments were meted on men caught smoking cigarettes, yet in the camp the ISIS fighters smoked. There seemed to be a significant amount of hypocrisy.

Akram was looking for a way to escape and return to home to his family. At that moment he decided becoming a suicide bomber gave him a better chance of escaping.

Akram chose his destiny, raising a hand to indicate his willingness to die for the caliphate.

There was much applause from his masters and everybody in the room.

Within a few days the soon-to-be martyr and a German volunteer were taken on a convoluted journey from Mosul to Baghdad.

Akram was passed from one Islamic State operative to another and stayed at various safe houses along the way. There was a week spent waiting in Falluja then finally Akram was delivered to an apartment in Baghdad. They immediately moved to another apartment and the young suicide bomber was told to take a nap. Two hours later, he was shaken awake.

'Wake up, wake up, it is time to put your vest on.'

Akram was given details of his target: a Shiite mosque in the neighbourhood of Bayaa.

A few hours later, at dusk, the nervous young man walked up to the gate of the mosque. He opened up his jacket.

'I'm wearing a suicide vest, but don't want to blow myself up. Please help me.'

A chaotic scene unfolded before a plain-clothes officer snipped off Akram's vest. The entire incident was captured on a bystander's smartphone and the footage swiftly distributed over social media. The YouTube video went viral, watched and shared by millions of people around the world.

Akram was led away by the police. After three weeks in custody and intensive interrogation he was released and returned to his home.

The End

Bibliography

http://scoutguidehistoricalsociety.com/bpbooks.htm

https://www.dosomething.org/facts/11-facts-about-child-soldiers

http://history.cass.anu.edu.au/monthinhistory/1914-monument-drought

http://en.wikipedia.org/wiki/2/21st_Battalion_(Australia)

https://www.awm.gov.au/units/unit_11272.asp?query=2%2F21+Battalion

http://www.civilwar.org/education/history/civil-war-overview/overview.html

http://army.gov.au/~/media/Files/Our%20future/LWSC%20Publications/SP/sp303_Developing_Australias_Maritime_Concept_of_Strategy-Michael%20Evans.pdf

http://en.wikipedia.org/wiki/Battle_of_Beersheba_%281917%29#Light_Horse_charge

http://www.secondworldwarhistory.com/fall-of-berlin.asp

http://www.history.com/topics/american-civil-war/battle-of-chattanooga

http://www.historynet.com/battle-of-chattanooga

http://www.history.com/topics/american-civil-war/battle-of-chickamauga

http://en.wikipedia.org/wiki/Battle_of_Fromelles

http://www.bbc.co.uk/remembrance/timeline/

http://www.bbc.co.uk/guides/zcvdhyc

http://www.bbc.com/news/uk-northern-ireland-30050870

http://www.bbc.com/news/world-europe-30134421

http://www.bbc.com/news/world-africa-13809501

http://newsweekly.com.au/article.php?id=4073

http://www.dailymail.co.uk/wires/aap/article-2676096/Boy-soldiers-answered-call-arms.html

https://www.awm.gov.au/encyclopedia/boysoldiers/first/

https://www.awm.gov.au/encyclopedia/boysoldiers/second/

http://www.independent.co.uk/news/world/boy-soldiers-using-children-in-warfare-is-not-a-modern-phenomenon

http://www.anzacs.net/BoySoldiers.htm

http://www.historylearningsite.co.uk/causes-american-civil-war.htm

https://scriptamus.wordpress.com/2009/11/02/child-soldiers-are-unfortunately-nothing-new/

http://civilwarsaga.com/child-soldiers-in-the-civil-war/

http://suffolkjournal.net/2014/11/child-warriors-tormented-as-they-are-forced-into-isis/

http://www.civilwar.org/education/history/children-in-the-civil-war/children-on-the-battlefield.html

http://www.civilwar.org/education/history/children-in-the-civil-war/civil-war-children.html

http://www.haileybury.com/co-curricular/co-curricular-life/combined-cadet-force

http://kerrincocks.blogspot.com.au/2014/11/of-poppies-and-potties.html

http://www.culteducation.com/group/1308-isis-the-islamic-state/28177-a-boy-in-isis-a-suicide-vest-a-hope-to-live.html

http://www.telegraph.co.uk/news/ww1-archive/11358011/Daily-Telegraph-January-23-1915.html

http://www.telegraph.co.uk/news/ww1-archive/11232219/Daily-Telegraph-November-16-1914.html

http://en.wikipedia.org/wiki/Dan_Bullock

http://edition.cnn.com/2012/10/08/world/africa/ishmael-beah-child-soldier/

http://www.ww2australia.gov.au/japadvance/laha.html

http://www.ww2australia.gov.au/japadvance/ambon.html

http://leadership.ng/features/410423/fight-boko-haram-turning-children-soldiers-spies

http://www.thefullwiki.org/First_Battle_of_Passchendaele

http://en.wikipedia.org/wiki/First_Battle_of_Ypres

http://histclo.com/essay/war/ww1/peo/cons/eng/w1e-boyv.html

http://www.firstworldwar.com/battles/ypres1.htm

http://tonyblairfaithfoundation.org/religion-geopolitics/commentaries/backgrounder/five-questions-onboko-haram

http://www.historytoday.com/ian-scott/heroin-hundred-year-habit

http://en.wikipedia.org/wiki/History_of_London

http://invisiblechildren.com/conflict/history/

http://histclo.com/youth/youth/org/nat/hitler/hitlera.htm

http://histclo.com/youth/youth/org/nat/hitler/act/warw/hja-war.htm

http://www.haileybury.com/honour/

http://www.dailymail.co.uk/news/article-2558424/Inside-Hitler-Youth-camps-youngsters-brainwashed-Nazis.html

http://en.wikipedia.org/wiki/James_Martin_(Australian_soldier)#Honours_and_awards

http://www.telegraph.co.uk/news/worldnews/africaandindianocean/uganda/10621792/Konys-child-soldiers-When-you-kill-for-the-first-time-you-change.html

http://www.hsph.harvard.edu/news/magazine/child-soldiers-betancourt/

http://thomaswebbphoto.com/portfolio/konys-stolen-former-child-soldiers-of-the-lra/

http://greatwarphotos.com/tag/london-regiment/

http://www.militaryhistoryonline.com/wwii/articles/effectiveorganization.aspx

http://en.wikipedia.org/wiki/Military_use_of_children#World_War_I

http://en.wikipedia.org/wiki/Military_use_of_children

http://www.aljazeera.com/indepth/features/2014/05/nigerian-vigilantes-aim-rout-boko-haram

http://www.logos-publishing.com/Hitlerjugend-3.htm

http://www.prattfoundation-israel.co.il/?parkhistory/eng

http://www.worldwar1postcards.com/real-photographic-ww1-postcards.php

http://www.civilwar.org/battlefields/chickamauga.html

http://www.historylearningsite.co.uk/battle_of_fromelles.htm

https://www.awm.gov.au/encyclopedia/fromelles/

http://opinionator.blogs.nytimes.com

http://www.awm.gov.au/blog/2007/10/30/the-charge-of-the-4th-light-horse-brigade-at-beersheba/

http://www.echucamoama.com/the-echuca-story

http://www.oocities.org/dutcheastindies/ambon.html

http://www.eyewitnesstohistory.com/berlin.htm

http://www.greatwar.nl/frames/default-feared.html

http://www.greatwar.nl/frames/default-children.html

http://www.historyplace.com/worldwar2/hitleryouth/hj-boy-soldiers.htm

http://www.warchild.org.uk/issues/the-lords-resistance-army

http://news.yahoo.com/third-ww1-sailors-were-boys-study-084033542.html

http://www.bl.uk/world-war-one/articles/training-to-be-a-soldier

http://en.wikipedia.org/wiki/Walpeup

http://wwiboysoldiers.weebly.com/works-cited.html

http://www.worldwar1postcards.com/ww1-prisoners-of-war-postcards.php

http://www.brookings.edu/~/media/research/files/articles

http://www.brookings.edu/research/interviews/2006/06/12humanrights-singer

http://thinkafricapress.com/nigeria/youth-vigilantes-stand-boko-haram-cost

www.ingramcontent.com/pod-product-compliance
Lightning Source LLC
Chambersburg PA
CBHW030516020726
47494CB00004B/1124